ISBN-13: 9798439651108
ISBN-10: 1477123456

Cover design by: Art Painter
Library of Congress Control Number: 2018675309
Printed in the United States of America

For my wonderful family, who never let me give up.

To Emily Ann
Hope you enjoy.
love
Kate
x

PORTUM

Chapter 1 – Salutem – Rules and Rebellion

The huge central cave in Salutem was crowded as people jostled for position, the air hot and cloying, as it always was for these big events. The band were ready to take their places on stage, but first Commander Tolson must speak. He stood quietly for a moment, arms raised, demanding obedience, until silence crept through the crowd, until all were focused solely on him.

'Fellow citizens!' he began. His voice, amplified by the microphone, bounced around the bare, smooth walls of the cave, and echoed among the huge pipes which ran overhead. 'I have a few announcements before we enjoy *The Flaming Heroes* this evening.'

There were a few ragged cheers from the crowd as the drummer raised his sticks above his head. Tolson frowned, glaring over his shoulder, then continued with his announcements, which consisted of the usual propaganda about the outside world and its unsuitability for human life. Along with a reminder of the consequences for anyone venturing to see for themselves. They'd all heard the tales of people being imprisoned for months in the deep caves. Folk died down there. After what seemed to the crowd to be an unreasonably long time, Tolson ended his announcements with the one they'd all been dying to hear.

'Enough from me, enjoy your evening ladies and gentlemen.' He turned a little and waved his arm towards the waiting band, as if he alone had conjured them. '*The Flaming Heroes!*'

The cave erupted with loud cheering as a crash of guitars and drums signaled the start of the concert.

Towards the back of the crowd were a group of young people, pretending to dance and sing along with everyone else. However, along with the song lyrics a conversation was going on.

'I can feel it happening!' Fenella said, shaking her head and holding it with both hands, pretending to enjoy the music. Her long, dark hair flew out around her, masking her face and ensuring that she was given space by her companions. When she looked up, worried green eyes sought the faces of her friends. 'Tell me it's not just me,' she said.

'No, it's me too,' said Bertram. He was frowning as he jumped around, dancing along with the crowd. 'It's like Tolson's in my head telling me what to think!' His mousey brown hair flopped over his eyes and he swept it back with his usual impatient gesture. Brown eyes found Chris, looking questioningly at his friend.

Chris nodded, he could feel it too, a sense of false happiness with their life, their world, confined as they were, along with a desire to obey the rules and to behave in a quiet manner. He ran a hand over his short, spiky brown hair then, catching a guard watching him, he grinned, shook his head, and carried on dancing and singing along with the band.

The group of friends had suspected for some time that the population of Salutem were being subjected to subliminal messaging. The monthly music concerts, which catered to all tastes, seemed the obvious time for the conditioning to take place. They had noticed the subtle changes, both in themselves and others, after each of the concerts. It was more noticeable after they'd all ended up in the deep caves for a month for rule breaking. There was no escape from the concerts in Salutem. Noise travelled to the farthest corners of the system, although the mind programming didn't reach the very lowest levels. They had taken great care to ensure that the guards didn't notice any changes in their behaviour, no use letting the authorities know about the chink in their armour. This concert would even be heard in the distant plant room which housed the huge generators, and in the water and air treatment rooms.

Tonight, everyone was listening to the band, whether they wanted to or not. Along with the music, Chris and his friends were now sure they were also receiving their monthly dose of mind control from the rulers of the colony.

As the concert ended, people began making their way back to their living quarters, which were arranged on three levels, along tunnels which radiated off the central cave like spider legs. Your level denoted your rank. Top level was for the elite, the commanders and their families. The middle level housed the managers, the healers, the teachers and, if they were lucky and especially well behaved, the odd team leader. The lower level housed the workers. The caves here were smaller, much closer together and had no private washing facilities, unlike the higher ups. Regardless of your level, there were no doors, not even in the bathing rooms. Curtains were hung across the doorways in an attempt at privacy.

Fenella, Chris and Bertram, with their friends Archie and Baz, hung back a little, allowing the crowds to flow around them. They were shaking their heads as if trying to dislodge a troublesome thought.

'I could feel it, but I couldn't stop it.' Chris said. 'I've got a right pain in my brain now!'

'How can we avoid it without being detected?' asked Fenella.

'We could find their stupid subliminals and rip them out.' Baz offered, rubbing her forehead with a fist.

A member of the guards was watching them rather too closely. Chris subtly nudged his friends into silence. 'Come on,' he said with mock cheerfulness. 'The Heroes always give us a headache, it's why we love them so much!'

The others followed suit and headed for their home caves.

Gradually, silence descended in Salutem. The population happy in their beds.

The Commander was being passed a note containing some disturbing news about potential rebels. Rebels he thought had already been tamed. He sighed before issuing an order for the group to be put under close watch. They couldn't afford any major trouble, much less a breakout, which is what he suspected this particular group were about to attempt.

***

The following morning Chris, Fen and Baz were among the last into the food hall for breakfast. They picked up their trays and located Bertram, sitting down before any of them spoke. Bertram nodded a greeting, he was already almost finished with his meal.

'Oh, my head!' were the first words out of Fen's mouth. 'It's worse than when we found that ancient bottle of gin! Do you remember?'

'I do. Do you think it's worse cos we're aware of it?' Chris asked.

'Aware of the gin hangover?'

'No Fen, aware of the...you know.' Chris looked around warily but there was no one near them. Not that that mattered, it was said the walls had ears in Salutem, no conversation was ever truly private, someone was always listening. He was sure the rule to keep the walls bare of anything but official posters had something to do with it.

'Could be,' Baz said with her mouth full. 'We were trying to fight against it, no wonder we've all got headaches really.' She passed a hand over her closely cropped hair, grimacing as she rubbed at her left temple.

Fenella considered this, head on one side as she chewed. She waved a fork at Baz, nodding, making her ponytail bounce. 'I was followed last night too,' she confided. 'Someone, I'm not sure who he was, followed me all the way to my quarters. It was creepy. I looked out after I'd got ready for bed and he was still there. Just standing, watching.' She shivered, looking around for sympathy or support.

Baz patted her arm. 'It'll be nothing,' she said. 'You know what they're like, petrified we'll do something *dangerous.*'

'I'm done,' Bertram said, standing up. 'Fen, I'm sure it will be alright, just be careful today. See you shortly Chris.' He nodded to the group and left.

'So,' Chris continued, his eyes following Bert's progress through the dining hall. 'What next?'

Baz was about to reply when her expression suddenly darkened and she applied herself vigorously to the remains of her breakfast. Chris risked a glance over his shoulder and spotted a couple of the guards watching them.

'Right, that's me done.' Chris said standing up. 'I'll see you guys later.' He picked up his tray and took it to the end counter for cleaning.

Moments later Fen joined him, placing her tray next to his. As they walked past the guards she said. 'You have a shift this morning Chris?'

'Yeah, the water treatment plant just won't function without me. You know how Bertram relies on my assistance.' He grinned at his friend. 'See you after work?'

Fen nodded. 'Yeah, see you later. Take care my friend.' And with that she'd gone, trotting towards the medical caves where she and Baz worked, cleaning and washing and hoping for promotion.

***

Bertram was already in the plant room when Chris arrived. They nodded to each other and Chris went to change into his blue overalls. Checking his work detail for the day, he saw he was scheduled to work with his friend and sauntered over, calling cheery greetings to other workers as he went past. He held out his hand and

Bertram gripped his forearm, the usual Salutem greeting. Bertram's overalls were red, indicating his supervisor status. The sleeves were already rolled up, revealing strong but very pale arms.

'What we got here then bro? Anything interesting?' Chris asked, rolling up his own sleeves.

'Dunno mate,' Bertram grunted. 'Summats stuck.' He hefted a huge spanner and brought it down heavily onto a pump casing, which rang loudly. A gurgle was followed by a plume of water and the two young men scrambled to contain it.

'What did you make of the concert last night?' Chris asked after the initial panic was over.

'Interesting,' Bertram responded. 'I'm so sure they're lying to us all, but I can't fathom out why. Father says none of it's true, of course, that we're just making it up, but I'm sure he just wants to stop us getting into any more trouble.'

'He's always like that, it's working for Tolson for all these years.' Chris said. 'It doesn't make any sense though, does it? I mean, why are they so mad keen on us all staying stuck in these caves? What's wrong with outside? Cos, I don't believe what they say about the old nuclear war, surely radiation doesn't hang about for that long?'

Bertram shrugged, then bent almost double trying to reach underneath the pump for a bolt. 'Wouldn't have thought so bro,' he grunted. 'Ah, gotcha!' He stood up holding the bolt triumphantly. 'This is the little beggar that's been causing the trouble, I'm sure of it!' He delved inside the pump mechanism, carefully feeling his way around for the home of the bolt.

Knowing what was coming, Chris readied the new nut and gave it to Bertram when his hand appeared expectantly.

'Switch her on,' Bertram said as he stood up, wiping his hands on the cloth he always had tucked into his back pocket.

Obediently, Chris reached for the switch and flicked it. Nothing happened for a moment, then a horrible grinding noise began. Hurriedly he pressed the switch off again and grimaced at Bertram.

Bertram sighed and slapped the pump with his now damp, grubby cloth. 'Looks like we'll be stripping this one right down,' he said. 'So much for a quiet day!'

Chris grinned, he enjoyed this sort of work, it was like a puzzle to him and he took satisfaction in making all the pieces fit together and work smoothly. 'Ah, you know we love doing jobs like this,' he said. 'It's our thing.' Bertram grinned in response.

Under cover of all the clangs and clunks which accompanied stripping down the motor, Chris and Bertram quietly discussed the previous evening and guessed at the reasons for keeping the population underground.

'Could be some sort of power trip,' Bertram suggested. 'But why keep at it for so long?'

'Yeah, what's in it for them?' Chris wondered. 'I mean, it's not like we're any threat to them, we don't wanna take over or anything, we just need to know what's out there, right?'

Bertram nodded, then swore quietly as a spring pinged off into the corner. Chris followed it and, while he was searching, he heard something strange. Bertram was making noises at the pump, unscrewing things and dropping them onto a tray, but it wasn't that. Chris froze and concentrated, leaning against the wall.

He heard it again. A whisper.

He stood up and signaled wildly until Bertram noticed him and stopped what he was doing, looking quizzically at him. Chris put a finger to his lips and gestured him over.

Sighing, Bertram straightened up and wandered over to his friend. Much to his astonishment, Chris pushed Bertram's head against the wall, and he was about to stand upright again when he heard it. His eyes widened as he looked at Chris, but he said nothing.

'*So, I said to them, I said I'm not doing it. Why would I spy for them?*'

Bertram took Chris by the arm and led him away from the corner, back to the pump, much of which now lay in pieces on the floor.

'Bro! What was that?' he murmured.

'No idea, more to the point, *who* was that?' he asked quietly. 'And who have they been asked to spy on? And who did the asking?'

'Exactly!' Bertram gave a particularly stubborn nut and bolt an extra heave and they groaned as they began to move. 'I'll be glad when we've got this all stripped,' he said more loudly. 'Must be years since this one had a good clean.'

Chris followed his example, 'Yeah, we'll soon have it all nice and shiny and working like a dream. Now, where did that spring go?'

He wandered off again, found the spring and couldn't resist putting his ear to the wall one more time.

'*...noisy. Something about a pump. Nothing of interest.*'

Chris felt his stomach churn. He headed back to Bertram.

'Found it!' He declared loudly and let the spring drop into the tray with the other pieces, ready for cleaning. 'It's us!' he said softly. 'I think they're spying on us!'

Bertram looked surprised but said nothing, he didn't need to make a noise, his face said it all. 'Well done you,' he said instead. 'We'd have been lost if you hadn't managed to find that. Soon be done now.' Under his breath he added. 'My father won't like this! I'll tell him later, he'll put a stop to it.'

They continued working in silence for a while, the only sounds were of nuts, bolts and other small but essential parts being dropped into the tray. Then Bertram let a small nut go, he didn't so much drop it as fling it towards the wall. He looked meaningfully at Chris, who nodded and scampered after it. Leaning down to locate the nut, he let himself rest against the wall. Bertram paused, watching him. Chris retrieved the nut and shook his head. Nothing.

'I bet this is cos of last night,' Chris said quietly. 'I noticed one of the guards watching us.'

'Yeah, Fen said she'd noticed too, and she was followed back to her quarters. Odd!' Bertram sighed, shaking his head.

11

'And your father insists there's nothing strange going on?'

When their shift was finished, they walked back towards their living quarters together, obviously tired and covered in grease.

'Must have been about us, they mentioned pumps. Who do you think it was?' Chris asked as they entered the main cavern where other noise would mask their conversation.

'No idea, but it was definitely female,' Bertram replied.

Chris nodded, 'We're going to have to be very careful,' he said. 'If we don't want another stint down below. But I want to know what's going on, don't you?'

Bertram nodded, then said rather more loudly than necessary, 'I reckon we did well today, at least we got that pump all stripped and began cleaning. We'll get it back together tomorrow. Thanks for your help. See you after you've had a shower!' He waved his hand beneath his nose as if the smell emanating from Chris offended him, grinning all the time, then turned and headed off for his own accommodation. Chris watched him go, then set off for his own family's rooms. He noticed a woman watching him. Her jacket bore the insignia of the Governors. He caught her eye and smiled cheekily at her. She dropped her gaze and walked away quickly. He watched her go, wondering.

***

Later that evening, as Chris sat with his parents for their evening meal, he glanced around the crowded dining hall.

'Chris, focus please. You're with us now, eat your food before it gets cold. We don't want it wasted.' His mother scolded him.

'Sorry Mum, I was just looking for Bertram and the others.' Chris tried to look apologetic and forced his attention back to the rapidly cooling, unappealing food on his plate. He hadn't spotted his friends, but he had noticed the woman again, sitting two tables away from his family. She had no plate in front of her, just a cup, and was watching him intently. Her eyes slid away from him every time he looked in her direction.

As the family finished their meal, Chris gathered up all the plates and stacked them neatly before taking them to the end table for cleaning. His elder sister used to do this, but she had recently been granted living quarters for herself and her partner and she was now expecting their first child. Population numbers were strictly controlled, and she would only be allowed to have two children, so he hoped she was enjoying her pregnancy, although the last he'd heard she was throwing up all the time. He was so glad he'd been born male.

After discharging his duties as the only child left with their parents, he sauntered off to find his friends. He spotted Fen and Baz at the other side of the hall and waved at them, but they didn't see him and left, heading for the entertainment area.

'Looks like it's just us this evening mate,' said a voice by his ear.

Chris jumped and looked round into Archie's broadly grinning face. Bertram stood just behind him.

Chris grinned. 'Fancy a game of cards?' he enquired. When they nodded he began the struggle to leave the dining hall, squeezing between tables and benches before finally making it to the huge archway which served as a doorway.

The friends made their way to the entertainment area and grabbed a small table in the corner. Archie produced a pack of playing cards and, as he shuffled, he looked around the room casually.

'So, how was your day in the waterworks?' he asked.

Bertram and Chris rolled their eyes and began telling him all about the stubborn pump. Bertram was about to mention the voice they had heard but Chris put a hand on his shoulder and leaned towards him, shaking his head slightly. He glanced over towards the door. The woman he had seen watching him at evening meal was standing there, scanning the room. Her eyes met his. She immediately lowered her gaze and walked out again.

'Was that her?' Bertram asked, very quietly.

'I think so,' Chris replied. 'I've caught her watching me a couple of times now.'

'Watching you?' Archie queried.

Chris nodded and between them, he and Bertram very quietly told Archie what had happened in the pump room.

They had been playing cards for half an hour before Fen and Baz found them. The girls drew up chairs and invited themselves to play. Chris dealt them in, and they continued to play quietly, until Fenella noticed their subdued behaviour.

'What's up with you three? You look like someone died!'

'Nothing, nothing wrong at all.' Chris said, glancing quickly around. 'Except,' he lowered his voice so that the girls had to lean closer to hear him. 'Except that Bertram and I overheard someone saying they'd been asked to spy on us, and now this strange woman keeps watching me!'

He watched with satisfaction as their expressions slid from horror to anger.

'That's terrible!' Fen exclaimed. Bertram and Chris shushed her.

'Keep your voice down Fen,' Bertram urged. 'We have to be careful. We don't know what they heard before, but they must have heard us talking or they wouldn't have put someone onto us. Although father still insists we're being ridiculous. I spoke to him while we were eating and he got angry, but with me, not them!' Bertram sounded peeved and a frown wrinkled his brow.

Fen put her hand over her mouth, her eyes wide.

'Makes you wonder, doesn't it,' Chris said casually as he shuffled the cards ready for the next hand. 'If we're onto something. You know, questioning everything?' He swiftly dealt the cards and the others picked them up.

Bertram nodded, his eyes on his cards. 'Like I said this morning, why would they lie? What's in it for them? What are they hiding?' He drummed his fingers on the table, frowning.

Chris sighed, 'No idea, but there must be something, or why bother?' He played his card, picked up another and groaned as he added it to his collection. 'This hand's terrible, I've got no chance with it.'

'You said that the other week,' Baz reminded him with a broad grin, displaying her missing front tooth. 'Then you beat us all, so I'm not sure I trust you.'

The group laughed and relaxed a little. Chris stretched and leaned back against the wall. He froze as he heard the whispers. Bertram noticed his face and began talking more loudly to the rest of the group. Chris rubbed a hand across his face, pretending to be more tired than he was, just in case he'd been observed. He drew himself up in his chair again and reviewed his cards.

'It's like a running commentary on what we're doing,' he said softly as he selected a card to play. 'We are most definitely being watched, and it's not just me, it sounds like it's all of us, so be careful please.'

Fenella's head shot up when he said this, a worry creasing her brow. Baz looked unconcerned, but then, not much seemed to have an impact on her.

'Maybe...perhaps...we should...you know...stop talking about...things. For a bit at least.' Archie stuttered nervously, his Adam's apple bobbing up and down. 'I...I don't want to end up in the deep caves again.' His mousey hair was always straggly, but tonight it resembled a collection of rats tails hanging round his face where he'd been worrying at it.

'No Arch, I won't be told what to think anymore!'

They all looked at Fenella in astonishment, she wasn't usually so strident.

'What? Well, I'm fed up of it, that's all. Now that I know it's happening, I want to know why, like really know why. What are they hiding?' She belatedly lowered her voice. 'Is it really that bad outside? Or are they keeping us in here for other reasons?'

'Like what?' Baz demanded. 'What reasons could they possibly have for keeping us in these stinking caves if the outside world is actually safe?'

This wasn't the first time they'd had this conversation, but never this publicly. Chris and Bertram began glancing around nervously. The girls weren't being quiet and those on the nearest tables were looking in their direction.

Chris sagged in his seat and leaned on the wall again.

'I've got a headache,' he announced. 'Wall's nice and cool.' He winked at Bertram who carried on as normal.

'*...the girl with long hair looks like the ringleader. The other girl...well, we already know about her...*'

'Shall we talk about something else?' Chris suggested brightly.

'Ok, like what?' Archie asked suspiciously.

'Oh, I don't know, anything really.' Chris said, looking earnestly at Bertram.

Bertram picked up on the cue and began talking about water pumps with Archie, who wasn't in the least bit interested but who couldn't get a word in edgeways once his friend got started.

Fen dealt the cards and took the opportunity to

hiss at Chris.

'What's all this about?'

'They think you're the ringleader,' he whispered back. 'Be careful. They say they already know about Baz too.' Although, in his opinion, Baz did herself no favours in that department with her razored hair, all black clothing festooned with strange bits of chain, the pin through her nose and her belligerent manner.

Fen looked surprised but said nothing, instead leaning back and surveying her cards. She nodded slowly, as if considering her hand.

'Ok. Right then.' She made her first play and the game continued.

Several more times during the evening, Chris leaned against the wall, each time he heard a snippet, but gradually they became more commonplace as the friends made a point of talking about work and family and concentrated on their game.

As they stood to leave, Chris, who had been thinking hard all evening and had consequently lost every game, spoke to the group. 'I reckon we need to see for ourselves you know.'

'See what?' Bertram asked.

'Outside. See if they're lying. Find out the truth.'

'How?' Fen asked as they strolled through the tables and towards the doorway.

'You know the service tunnel? The big one? Well, I'm pretty sure it leads to the outside, that's why we're banned from going up that way.' Chris said. 'That's why you need staff passes to get up there.'

The group drew to a halt in the middle of the communal hallway, apparently to say their goodnights.

'We'll discuss it tomorrow morning.' Bertram said, his voice quiet but firm.

'Fair enough.' Chris conceded calmly, though his insides were fizzing with excitement. If they were going to do this, they needed plans in place.

The five friends wished each other good night and headed off to their beds.

**

After a sleepless night, Chris wandered drowsily towards his breakfast. Picking up his tray, he looked around for his friends. They weren't there yet so he made his way to a table in the middle of the dining hall and began eating. A heavy thump on his shoulder interrupted him and he turned to grin at Bertram, waving his fork in greeting.

Bertram sat down and began inspecting his breakfast. He was halfway through a piece of toasted bread from which he had picked several spots of blue mold, when Archie arrived, panting.

'Fen's gone!' he announced dramatically.

'What do you mean gone?' Chris demanded.

'Gone. Like…gone.'

'Taken you mean?' Bertram asked.

'I dunno!' Archie said helplessly. 'I went to call for her to come to breakfast and she wasn't there, and her Mum said she'd…gone.'

Concern for their friend creased Chris' brow, things had taken a serious turn now.

'What about Baz?' Bertram asked.

Archie shrugged, he hadn't thought of her.

As they finished their breakfasts, Baz appeared at their table and plonked down her tray. She sat, then noticed their expressions. 'What?' she asked as she began her meal. 'Where's Fen?'

With a sigh Chris quietly explained and watched as her normally pale face turned grey.

'So, they're serious then?' she said, pushing the plate away from her.

'It looks like it. Best keep our heads down today.' Bertram suggested.

With nods of agreement, they all rose and made their way to their various employments.

***

After a day spent reassembling the water pump they'd previously stripped back, Chris and Bertram met once again after their evening meal, keen to see if anyone had news and eager to impart their own. Baz and Archie followed them to the same card table as the previous evening.

'Any news?' asked Chris.

Baz shook her head.

'Not a whisper,' Archie replied with a wry little smile. 'She's just vanished.'

'We've heard nothing today either,' Chris confirmed. He'd spent the day making regular trips to the walls to check for voices. 'I was starting to think I was imagining it all, but then that woman turned up in the pump room.'

Archie looked horrified. 'Why?'

'Oh, she was complaining to the boss about water pressure or something, in the kitchens. He told her it was because we'd had to strip and rebuild one of the pumps, but that it would all be sorted by this evening.'

'But it was her? Do you think she was checking up on you?' Baz said, getting right to the heart of the matter.

'Probably, but we were busy working, didn't hardly glance up when she walked in.'

'Look,' Bertram's voice was quiet but intense. 'I reckon Chris is right, we need to get out of here, to see for ourselves what's going on. It's obvious to me that there's something wrong now. I mean, Fen hasn't disappeared for no reason, even her parents don't know where she is!'

'Of course they do!' Baz said, her eyes blazing. 'They've been threatened not to tell us. It's a warning is what it is, trying to make us behave.'

'Not working then, is it?' Bertram said fiercely. 'I even asked my father about her earlier, and he said he didn't know anything, but I could tell that he does, his eyes were very shifty. He just told me to make sure I be-have myself.' Bertram spat out the final few words, his eyes blazing.

'Tomorrow morning?' Chris asked, his eyes bright with excitement.

'Tomorrow morning, bro,' Bertram nodded. 'At the start of the big tunnel. 5am sharp, right?'

The rest of the group nodded eagerly, ready for adventure.

Chapter 2 - Escape

At 5am the following morning, Chris stood at the arranged spot, waiting. By quarter past he was getting worried. Then he heard shouts that sounded like Baz and Archie. He heard loud voices which sounded like authority. And heavy boots headed in his direction.

He looked up the tunnel, then back towards the noises. Thoughts of his family flashed across his mind. He knew the price he would pay for doing this, but he had to know. The only way he could save his friends was to find out the truth.

He turned and ran up the tunnel, towards the outside world and freedom.

Chris ran around a bend in the tunnel and stopped. Panting, he leaned against the wall but heard nothing, felt only the cold, damp stone. Bending double, his hands on his knees, he tried to catch his breath. At the sound of booted feet approaching, he turned and, still breathing heavily, began his ascent once more

He caught glimpses of tunnels leading from either side of the main passage. There were dim lights set in the walls and he could see a series of doorways, each sealed with wood. But he had no time to look, he had to keep going, or all would be lost, for all of them. He would be caught and left to rot in the deep caves.

The huge, heavy wooden door was in sight now. The sound of boots seemed further away. Perhaps they were having trouble with the steep incline in their heavy equipment.

Breathing heavily, he arrived at the door. It was as tall as two grown men and four times as wide. Fortified with iron, in the dim light from the wall sconces he could see the huge bolts which kept the population confined, or the outside world at a safe distance, depending on which story you listened to.

Footsteps were approaching. Chris froze, reaching for the blade in his belt which would ensure extra time in the caves if he were caught. But these were not the heavy boots of the guards, this was a much lighter tread. He could hear panting.

'Chris! Wait!'

It was Bertram, exhausted, running as fast as he could towards him.

'They got the others, but I wasn't where I was supposed to be.' Bert grinned through his panting, leaning against the wall. He held out his hand, which Chris gripped in their usual salute. Bertram nodded at the doors. 'We doing this then?'

Chris returned the grin and touched the bolts. No alarm, which he thought strange when you considered how paranoid the Elders were about escapees. Carefully, he slid back the first bolt, then the second. Someone had greased them, they ran smoothly. He turned the huge round handle and together they pulled, grunting with effort. The heavy door swung open noiselessly.

There was a rush of warm, fresh air and a brightness which their eyes had never seen. Squinting and shielding them with their hands, they stepped out of the door and into the world for the first time. Green filtered through their fingers. They kept their eyes lowered. A well-worn path led away from the door towards a cliff face.

'Hey, look,' Chris pointed. 'Wonder what that's all about?'

'Supplies?' Bertram guessed. 'Oh come on Chris, you can't be surprised that they know what's out here. They just don't want us to know about it.'

'Yeah, I guess, but why? I mean look at it!' Chris gestured to the lush greenery around them.

Bertram shrugged. 'Who knows? They're all control freaks. Thing is, we know now, we can tell people!'

They looked at each other as big grins spread over their faces.

'We did it!' They said together, embracing each other. Bertram slapped Chris on the back and he felt tears welling in his eyes.

Their celebrations were cut short as they heard footsteps approaching. The heavy step of the guards. Quickly they ran and hid beneath some huge, green, flat, things. Peering between the greenery the two young men watched as a group of guards emerged and looked around. They were shouting to someone in the tunnel, then they turned and went back inside.

Then came the sound of the door being firmly shut and the bolts being shot back.

'Well that's that then.'

'How are we going to get back in and tell everyone the truth?' asked Chris.

'We're not. That's the point. Well, it's their point.'

Bertram sank to the floor.

'We've got to try!' Chris took a few steps back towards the doors.

'Don't bother bro, you heard them being locked. There's no chance.'

'But they can't just leave us out here to die!' Chris was starting to panic.

'They can, they have.'

'Why?' Chris wailed.

'Because they don't want us going back in and disrupting everything. If we tell folk the truth what hold do the Leaders have over them?'

Bertram stood and looked around him, fighting to remain calm. He had to do this, to try, for Fen. How else could he hope to get her out? Looked like Chris needed his leadership too, as usual. 'Bro, at least we're not rotting in those bloody caves,' he said, trying to sound confident and strong. 'We're out here, in the light and the air and the … whatever these things are.' He pointed at the plants surrounding them.

Chris thought of Fen. At least she wasn't alone. Baz and Archie would be with her, or at least near her. He knew it was possible to talk to each other down there. He squared his shoulders. He could do this. He'd find a way to get back in and save her, save them all. He clapped Bertram on the back as, eyes adjusting to the light level, they looked around.

Bertram saw the change in Chris and nodded his approval. 'Let's head this way.' He indicated a narrow pathway twisting between the greenery.

It looked as good as any other direction, so they began walking, keeping as close to each other as possible. Each strange noise startled them and they both kept looking over their shoulders, half expecting pursuit. The floor was covered, for the most part, in something green, fibrous and springy, it reminded Chris of the moss he'd been made to scrub off the walls in the water treatment cave. He'd hated that scrubbing brush; he rubbed his knuckles as he recalled the bruising they had suffered.

There were lots of the flat, green things and, above them on long, thin, green sticks were bright plate-like structures, each with a long, thin, bright yellow tongue. Chris knew vaguely what leaves were, he had been required to visit the hydroponics stations whilst at school, but these huge, bright things bore little resemblance to the spinach and lettuce he'd seen growing in Salutem.

Even the roof supports out here were strange.

'Hey Bertram, these are weird,' cried Chris, slapping one of the straight, brown supports. 'They're not like the ones we used in the back caves, you know, where the roof almost fell down on that guy's head?'

Bertram looked back, and then looked up. Chris followed his gaze.

'Not sure these have much to support bro,' said Bertram. He tried to keep the wobble out of his voice.

Chris gulped but made himself keep looking.

'There's no roof,' he said slowly. 'Just that bright blue cover thing. Can't see what it's made of though, too far away. These things must be longer than the ones back home.' He slapped the support, which moved very slightly. 'Not properly secured either!' Chris hurried the next few steps, so he was right behind Bertram.

The lights were turned up fully too. It was very bright, even among the green leaves. And it was hot.

'What a waste of power, they should turn that down a bit.'

'What?' Bertram looked questioningly at Chris. 'What did you say?'

'Just that it's too much light and heat. They should turn it down a bit.'

'Not sure it works like that out here.' Bertram glanced up, squinting through the green canopy. 'Not seen any cables anywhere.'

Slowly, without realising what they were doing or where they were going, the boys made their way further into the greenery, away from the doors. They had been wandering for a long time when a noise made them jump. They turned to see a creature watching them. It was the size of a canine pup and covered in rough, spiky look-ing hairs, like a brush. It made a grunting noise. As they stared at it, it turned and trotted off.

'What was that?' Chris said quietly.

'No idea bro,' Bertram replied. 'Hope it hasn't gone to fetch its big brothers.' He gave a nervous half laugh.

The supports ahead seemed to thin out and the ground was more even. Chris and Bertram stepped out into a clear space. The floor was still covered in the green moss-like stuff, but it was different here, it was softer and waving in the air conditioning. All around were brightly coloured little balls, held aloft on green sticks. In the middle of the space was a much larger version of the creature they'd seen earlier. Around it were several of the small ones, all making the grunting noises and wandering about as if they had no cares at all.

Chris and Bertram crouched low to the ground and watched them. A movement on the far side of the space caught their attention and they froze. A large, spotted creature, a huge version of the cats kept in the caves, was watching the grunters. Watching them very carefully, creeping towards them.

'That's like the cats Gordy has in the stores to catch mice and rats,' Chris whispered, using his sleeve to wipe sweat from his forehead.

'Only lots bigger!' Bertram nodded, keeping his eyes firmly on the huge cat.

As they watched, horrified, it leapt on the grunters and caught one of the small ones, which squealed loudly. The larger grunter turned and bellowed at the huge spotted cat, charging towards it at a speed which surprised the watchers. It lowered its head and opened its mouth, revealing large yellow teeth. The cat was obviously alarmed as it dropped its prey and ran away. The big grunter ran after it a way, bellowing, before returning to the young. After much fussing, all the small ones gathered close to their parent and they moved away together into the dense greenery beneath the supports and their green, leafy, wavy roof.

With even more care than before, keeping close together and making a point of looking all around, Bertram led the way across the space and into the dense area of supports. They heard water running nearby and headed towards it.

'You thirsty?' Chris asked quietly.

'Parched,' Bertram replied. 'Doubt there'll be a tap handy out here though.' He tried to laugh but the sound got lost in his throat and came out as a cough instead.

'Alright?' Chris asked, concern written on his face as he patted his companion on the back. Bertram just nodded, his eyes were watering now and he hung his head, not wanting Chris to think he was weak or scared.

Stepping carefully between the supports, holding onto them where necessary to prevent themselves from slipping as the ground became muddy and began to slope, they slowly made their way towards the sound of water. After a few minutes of slipping and sliding they stepped out into another clear space. But this one went on for a long, long way.

'Oh my!' Bertram breathed, his hand reaching for Chris.

'I never thought it would be so big out here.' Chris put his arm loosely around Bertram and clasped his shoulder.

'Scared?' Bertram gave a cheeky grin, his head cocked on one side.

'A little,' Chris admitted. 'Starting to wonder if we were mad to do this.' He was trying hard not to notice that there was no roof out here, and the walls seemed a very long way away.

'Of course we're mad!' Bertram laughed loudly. 'But out here being mad is better than staying in there,' he jerked a thumb back over his shoulder. 'Locked up and going insane.'

Chris nodded, 'I suppose so.' He forced his reluctant gaze to return to the vista in front of them. As far away as he could see were rugged, rough shapes, green and grey with patches of white on their tops. Closer to him was lots of flat greenery, speckled with blue patches, the odd support standing alone, which Chris knew was madness, and the water they'd heard. It was not in an enclosed pipe, as he was used to, but open to the roof. Like someone had left the top half of the pipe off. But the pipe was all bent and twisted. It was obvious to Chris that it lacked the proper support and needed some work to rectify the problems.

'This needs some work,' he said to Bertram. 'It's all bent.'

'Hardly surprising,' Bertram replied. 'There's no top on it.' He looked around. 'Perhaps we could fix it,' he said, eyeing up a nearby branch and giving it a kick with his boot.

Chris was looking down into the water as it flowed past and saw things in it, darting about.

'That's not fit to drink!'

'What's up?' Bertram asked, dragging his eyes back to the water in front of him.

'There's things living in that!' Chris pointed to the fish he could see in the river.

'We've gotta find something to drink soon,' Bertram said, 'it's so hot out here.'

'And some food,' Chris said, rubbing his belly. 'We left before breakfast.'

Bertram nodded vaguely; he was looking to his

right where the water flowed from. There was nothing apart from flat green on the other side of the water and supports on this side. Turning, he looked to his left, watching the water flow away from him.

'How do we get across this?' he wondered out loud.

'Across? Why?' Chris was looking at the huge expanse over the water. 'There's nowhere to hide over there.'

'Not sure we need to hide bro,' said Bertram quietly. 'I'm sure they haven't followed us. We've not heard anything, and those guards aren't known for their gentle tread!'

They laughed and Bertram slung his arm around Chris' shoulders.

Then they heard voices.

Chapter 3 - Outsiders

Darting back under cover, they crouched, waiting. Expecting to be captured and dragged back to Salutem. Bertram kept a hand on Chris' shoulder, not sure which of them needed this reassurance the most.

'Guards,' Bertram said softly, listening to the approaching voices. But they sounded too cheerful to be guards. He couldn't make out what they were saying yet.

'Maybe.' Chris said. 'Should we let them catch us?'

'What? Why?' Bertram looked at him in amazement.

'I know we'd be punished, and they'd make an example of us. But at least there's food and water there,' Chris said in a rush. 'And our parents could come see us, maybe,' he finished lamely.

Bertram shook his head. 'I've not come this far to give up now,' he said firmly. 'I'm not giving them the satisfaction of dragging me back there! Besides, I'm pretty sure my father will have disowned me by now, he won't want to risk his rank.'

The voices were drawing closer now.

'I think,' Bertram said slowly. 'That they are not guards.'

His face crinkled as he thought for a moment then, decision made, he stood and stepped out into the clear area next to the water, mud oozing around his boots. He stood still, looking towards the voices, surely he would see them any moment.

'Bertram!' Chris gasped, 'No! You'll be seen!'

Bertram shrugged and, after a moment's thought, Chris joined him, standing close to him, staring nervously upstream.

As they watched, a strange object came into sight and floated towards them on the water. It was wide, flat and long, and there were people sitting on it. They were definitely not guards. These people were dressed very differently, draped in rough woven green fabric and something that looked like it may have come from the spotted creature he'd seen earlier. The men and women all had long hair.

Terrified, Chris took a step back into his hiding place, but Bertram stood still, and they saw him. They cried and waved, a couple jumped from their seats into the water and ran towards him.

Bertram stood frozen, his eyes wide as he looked at the strangers, not at all confident that he'd done the right thing. Hands grasped his arms, although not unkindly, and he was pulled closer to the water. Bertram looked back for Chris. 'Come on Chris,' he yelled.

The strangers looked, spotted Chris and ran back to grab him and pull him from his hiding place, dragging him towards the water where Bertram stood, being held firmly by the newcomers.

'Oh well done,' he muttered fiercely as he was forced to join Bertram. 'This is just perfect, now we're gonna get eaten by savages!'

One of their captors, a tall muscular man with large, black, banded tattoos on both upper arms, lifted a long stick. Chris, panic stricken, jerked himself free from those holding him. With no time for thought, he swung for the man holding the stick and punched him heavily on the nose. Blood gushed from the man's nose and he dropped his stick. He looked furiously at Chris, raised his arms as if to retaliate but, amid many shouts and much arm waving by his companions, instead he retrieved the stick and threw it back in the direction Chris and Bertram had taken. There was a lot of snarling and growling and both young men turned to see the spotted cat, the stick stuck firmly in its chest. As they watched, the creature sagged, became quiet and lay perfectly still.

'T'was close,' the man holding his arm said. 'You'm was nearly dinner there my lads,'

'Sorry?' said Bertram.

Chris was horrified, staring at the cat. It looked like the same one they'd seen earlier failing to catch a grunter. It had missed its meal. He understood the word dinner.

'Yon Jaguar was lookin' ta eat'cha.' The man looked down at them, his eyes crinkled. 'You from yon caves?'

'Caves? Yes, we come from Salutem.' Chris eagerly caught onto the familiar word. 'Dinner? It was going to eat us?'

The man nodded and Chris looked again at where the creature lay, perfectly still. The stick thrower, his nose still bleeding, was kneeling by the creature now, one hand on its head, his own head bowed. Chris noticed he kept wiping at his face with his free hand.

'What's he doing?'

'He's thanking it.'

'For not killing us?' Chris considered this to be odd

behaviour indeed but thought it kind of the stranger.

'Nah lad, for giving its life. We'll eat for days now, and we have a fine new pelt.'

Chris shook his head. He could understand some of the words the stranger was saying, but it made little sense to him. He looked questioningly at Bertram, who simply shrugged and shook his head.

'It didn't give its life, he took it.' Chris said, pointing to the man.

Beside him there was a sigh.

'They're always like this when they first come out.' A woman's voice said, close to Chris' left ear. 'Are you alright?' she said, carefully pronouncing each word. 'Want a drink?'

Chris nodded eagerly and was handed a strange, soft bottle. He stroked it wonderingly before the woman, laughing, removed the stopper. He lifted it to his nose to sniff cautiously at the contents.

'It's only water boy, drink!' the woman instructed.

He lifted it to his lips and took a sip. Clean, cool water. Chris drank deeply.

'Thanks.' Chris handed the bottle back to the woman, who then proffered it to Bertram. 'Who are you? I didn't think there were any people outside? We were told that the world was empty, ruined.'

'I am named Anilla,' she told him. 'We've come across your people before. We understand, but what you were told is not true. Obviously!' She waved a hand expansively at the surrounding greenery. 'What's your name?'

'Chris, I'm Chris, and he's Bertram,' he answered, indicating his friend who was quenching his thirst. Then his brain caught up. 'Wait! You say you've met more people from Salutem?'

Anilla nodded, 'And other caves too.' She turned to speak to her companions while beside her Bertram spluttered and Chris stood frozen, his mind whirling.

'There are other caves?' Bertram asked, handing the water skin back.

Anilla laughed, 'Yes, lots of them. Were you told your community was the only one? The only people to survive? What were you told happened?'

'We've gotta get going,' one of the men called. 'Else we'll miss the cave.'

'OK Farle, we're coming.' Anilla smiled at Chris and Bert, 'Come on, we can talk as we travel.'

'Where are you taking us?' Chris felt fear bubbling in his stomach. These people were strangers and they were taking him away from any hope of returning to his family. Could he trust them?

'Come on Chris,' said Bertram, pulling his arm. 'It's not safe here,' he indicated the dead cat, which was being bound and loaded onto the back of the floating platform. 'Let's go and see where they live.' Then he put his head close to Chris' and whispered. 'We can always get back; we'll just follow the water.' He pointed at the vessel. 'I think this thing can only move on the water, so we'll know which way to go.'

Chris nodded reluctantly.

'We need to get back to Portum. Come on, you'll be

safe with us.' Anilla hopped casually onto the flat platform. It made no sense to Chris and he was starting to shake his head when the man who had thrown the stick at the creature took him firmly by the arm and made him step onto it. The platform wobbled and Chris sat down very suddenly. Bertram laughed at him before stepping aboard himself and sitting beside his friend.

The group of strangers, laughing and chattering, arranged themselves on the benches and edge of the craft and then, assisted by two of the men using long poles, they began to float along on the flowing water. Anilla was sitting quietly, doing something with flat green blades she'd pulled from the ground.

Chris sat quietly for a few minutes, one hand shielding his eyes as he looked around him, glad of the comforting presence of Bertram. There were five outsiders and only two of them, they had little chance of escape and, he realised, they had no idea where the food was out here. There was certainly no dining hall, no entertainment lounge, no concerts. He felt a sudden pang of homesickness for the caves he had hated a few hours previously, and, to his horror, felt tears come to his eyes. He blinked furiously, lowering his head, hoping no one would notice. How could he admit that he wanted his mother? What would Bertram say if he told him that this was a horrible mistake? That he'd only intended to have a peek into the outside world, then scurry back inside and tell everyone what he'd seen. That he'd never wanted to *stay* out here, where there was no roof, no walls. He shivered; he could barely bring himself to look to his right at the vast green, empty space.

Anilla moved carefully to sit with the boys and

handed each of them a roughly woven hat with a broad brim. 'Wear these,' she instructed. 'The sun is strong and your skin isn't used to it.'

Chris and Bertram reluctantly took the items she handed to them, looking blankly at each other.

'Wear them?' Chris asked. 'Where? What is it?'

'They're hats!' Anilla laughed. 'You put them on your heads, surely you know what hats are?' The boys shook their heads and she sighed. 'They are to protect your heads and necks from the sun,' she pointed to the bright light which dangled from the blue cover which passed for a roof out here. 'It will burn you if you're not careful, and your skin is very pale from living underground.' She took the hat from Chris' hands and placed it on his head. 'There!'

Bertram hastily followed suit and he and Chris sat there with bright green foliage on their heads. They felt foolish, but when Chris reached up to remove the hat, Anilla gently smacked his hands and shook her head.

'They should turn it down,' Chris said, indicating the sun. 'If it's so hot it'll burn. Wasting power.'

Anilla shook her head, her eyes twinkling, then she smiled reassuringly at them. 'I know everything is so different out here, it must be scary,' she said gently. 'But I promise you are safe with us. Let me introduce you.' She sat up and began pointing to each of her companions in turn. 'This is Jax, he thinks he's the leader.' There was general laughter at this and the one named Jax shook his head and laughed too. This was the man who had thrown the stick, whose nose Chris had bloodied. He groaned, putting his new hat over his face, and Bertram grinned.

'Great start bro, beating on the leader!'

'This is Farle, and Ishy and Merel. Everyone, this is Chris and Bertram.' Anilla pointed to each of them as she carefully said their names, stuttering a little over Bertram.

'What is this thing?' Chris asked, patting the floating platform in which they sat in an effort to cover his embarrassment. 'And how does it stay up?'

Farle, an older man who wore a bushy beard and had a pattern of black tattoos down the whole of his left arm, grinned at him. 'Tis a boat lad, and the water holds it up.'

'Boat.' Bertram said the unfamiliar word slowly, then continued. 'Water can't hold things up! I worked with the water in the caves, it goes in pipes and...'

Anilla shrugged. 'I don't know how it works either,' she said carefully. 'But it does!'

'You an engineer then?' The one named Ishy asked. He was clean shaven and had only one tattoo on his upper arm. Chris thought he looked younger than the others.

'I... I don't know what that means,' Bertram was annoyed as he stuttered.

'Ah...er...you work with machines and the like?'

'Oh, yes!' Relief flooded Bertram's face. 'I worked on the filtration system and the pumps and stuff.' He looked up at the five blank faces and it was Chris' turn to grin.

'Machines that clean water and move it to where it's needed.'

The conversation stopped as the water was running faster now and it needed the full concentration of the team to keep the boat on course.

Anilla sat with Chris and Bertram and they talked quietly. She told them the names for the strange things they was seeing. They now knew that the roof supports were called trees. But the green things had many different names. All were plants she told them, but some were flowers and others were herbs. She indicated the various bundles of plants which were heaped around the boat. They were bound with strong, green leaves and gave off peculiarly pungent smells.

Chris felt his head starting to spin as Anilla continued speaking. She told them about the birds and animals there were seeing in the distance. She pointed out deer, and horses and they saw huge flocks of birds.

'We saw some other animals,' Chris told her, glad to be able to add something to their quiet conversation. 'Near where you found us. A big one and some little ones, they were hairy and they grunted.' He gave an impression of the noise the animals had made and Anilla threw her head back and laughed.

'Hogs!' she cried.

'Where?' Jax was suddenly on high alert, looking around.

'No Jax, they saw some earlier,' she said, wiping her eyes.

'What is this Portum you're taking us to?' Bertram asked.

'It's where we live,' she said. 'There are quite a few of us.'

'How far is it?' Bertram was beginning to feel flutters of nerves now. Although these people seemed nice enough, they could be anyone and they could be taking him and Chris anywhere. He must keep his wits about him, try to remember the way, just in case. He had to try and keep them safe.

'About two hours, then, once we're through the cave it's just getting to the other end.' Anilla said, as if this made it all clear. 'We should be there before it gets dark.'

'Dark? You mean someone puts the lights out for you?' Chris queried.

Anilla laughed and was about to explain, but just then a rumbling began. The water got spiky and all the trees and plants shook. Chris and Bertram grasped the sides of the boat and looked around with panic in their eyes.

'What's happening?' Chris gasped.

'Volcano.' Merel said, he was standing in the middle of the boat and looking back the way they'd come. 'I think it's gonna blow soon, we need to be as far away as we can.'

Chris looked at Anilla. 'Volcano?'

'It's a mountain.' She saw his blank expression. 'A hill?' She tried again. 'Like the ones over there.' She pointed to the distance where the rough shapes edged the flat greenery. As she spoke, the rumbling ceased.

Chris nodded slowly. 'What does he mean it's gonna blow?' he asked, attempting to imitate the way Merel had pronounced the words.

'Volcanos do that sometimes,' Anilla told him. 'They rumble like this, then there's an explosion...a big loud bang and it all breaks apart and really hot stuff comes out of it.'

'Oh!' Chris was surprised but prepared to believe anything in this strange new world.

'Sounds like that pump we fixed last week,' Bertram said, laughing nervously. 'Only bigger.'

The trees by the edge of the water, which they now knew to call a river, thinned and flat green stretched as far as they could see on both sides. Chris was torn between fascination for his new surroundings and terror at the lack of roof and walls. His eyes wanted to close, to deny what he was seeing, but his curiosity won. There were lots of animals by the side of the river, eating the green. When the rumbling and shaking began again, the animals looked around, startled, and began to run away, following the direction of the river and their boat.

Then came the loud bang Anilla had mentioned, much louder than anything they had heard before, and it went on for what felt like a long time. Bertram and Chris looked back to see a plume of smoke, big, thick and dark, rising high above the trees.

'Looks like when Chad's cooking,' Chris said to Bertram.

'Remember his spinach stew?' Bertram asked, pulling a face.

They watched the smoke as it rose up, higher and higher, making the light go darker. They looked at the outsiders, but they were relaxing now.

'It's alright,' Anilla said soothingly. 'It's too far away to hurt us.'

'It's blowing t'other way too,' Farle said. 'We'm not long from Portum now.'

Chris nodded, he was beginning to understand the way they spoke a little, but he was not happy at being taken so far from Salutem and his friends and family. He almost wished he'd been caught and taken to the lower caves with his friends, at least he knew what would happen to him there. And he'd be safe.

Bertram too was lost in thought. He was hungry and despite his earlier display of confidence, he was frightened. He wondered how far it was to Salutem from here, to his family, to Fen.

***

Chris was quiet as they continued their journey, he pretended to take great interest in the surrounding greenery, but if he was honest, he was getting bored with it. It served no purpose. Back in Salutem everything was there for a reason, walls and roof kept you safe, animals were for milk, eggs, wool and meat. Here there were trees that didn't support anything, exploding hills, animals, but what was the use of it all?

Right ahead of them was a big hill, they were getting closer and closer to it, until it loomed over them and the boat and the people in it felt tiny and vulnerable. It looked as if the water went right into the hill. He couldn't see how it was possible for them to stay on the boat, surely they would crash into the rocks? It was all too much. Panicking, he started to get up but Anilla put her hand on his leg and shook her head.

'It's alright Chris,' she said. 'The boys know what to do. It's quite safe. We've done this trip many, many times before.'

He looked at her fearfully, but she was so calm, smiling at him, that he chose to settle down again. He could always jump off before they crashed he decided, he was sure the water wasn't too deep for him to get to the edge safely.

There was more talk between the men now. Chris couldn't follow what they were saying, but they were manoeuvring the boat right into the middle of the river. As Chris watched, a gap appeared beneath the rocky hill ahead. He nudged Bertram with his elbow, pointing to the opening beneath the rock. Bertram nodded, he was mesmerised, watching the water level drop and the cave appear. Jax had stopped the boat by holding his long stick in the water. They were waiting.

Chris watched as the water slowly dropped. The gap was getting bigger all the time. Eventually, there was just enough room for the boat to be allowed to float, gently and carefully underneath the hill. Everyone crouched down as the boat slid into the gap. It was dark and wet, and Chris was dripped on quite a few times. He could feel his heart beating very fast in his chest, and he hardly dared breathe. Turning his head slightly, he could see light ahead of them.

No one spoke as the boat slowly drifted through the tunnel, but there were cheers when they emerged on the other side, slightly damp but none the worse for their experience.

Chris sat up, looked around him and gasped. Surrounding them now was more flat green, edged with hills, but these hills were bigger than the ones he'd seen earlier. There were lots of animals here, peacefully eating the green.

'Why do they eat the green?' he asked no one in particular.

'It's their food. They eats grass. It's what cattle do.' Farle explained. Chris could hear the smile in his voice. So, he thought, the flat green is called grass, and these chunky animals are cattle.

'Why don't they run away?' he asked.

'There's no way out,' Jax said behind him. 'Only way in and out of Portum is by river, through the cave. Or you have to fly!'

Chris had no idea what he meant, but the others were laughing. It made him feel uncomfortable, he hated not understanding. He looked questioningly at Bertram, who simply shrugged and shook his head, but, seeing that his friend needed support he slung his arm casually around his shoulders and gave him a gentle shake.

'It'll be alright, bro,' he whispered.

'But what does he mean, fly?' Chris was starting to shake now.

'Not a clue,' Bertram said, hoping his voice wouldn't wobble. 'But we're here now, and they all seem ok so far. Let's just see how things go shall we? I'm sure it'll all become clear in a while.'

Chris nodded miserably, he wished he could stop feeling dizzy. He was so hungry! His tummy was making embarrassing noises. He hugged himself in an effort to make it stop before people began noticing.

They floated on down the river and rounded a

bend. Now he could see how enormous this place was. The river split in two ahead of them, creating land in the middle. He could see buildings there, a couple of them huge, puffing out great towers of smoke. On the far-right hand side he saw more buildings scattered around, most of them well away from the water. There was a wooden construction across the river, Chris saw a group of people walking across it. As he watched they stepped down from the wooden walkway onto the stone path and trotted away to the hills at the far back of the area, from which came a series of loud bangs. Nervously he looked at Anilla, was this another volcano? But none of his companions were taking any notice, and there was no plume of smoke, so he relaxed again.

Flocks of birds flew overhead, coming to land on the river, Chris could hear them honking and quacking to one another. He watched them dipping their heads beneath the water, shaking droplets from their feathers as they resurfaced.

Jax steered their boat down the left-hand path and Chris saw a group of people. They appeared to be waiting for them. Behind them he could see buildings, clustered together, well back from the river. The buildings were made of stones at the bottom and timber above, with vegetation forming a roof. There were rather a lot of them. He felt afraid, felt a longing for his family cave, for the familiar sounds and smells. For solid stone walls and a roof. For safety.

The river had less water here, and there was gravel visible underneath it. Jax and Ishy leapt out of the boat and hauled it onto the sandy gravel at the side of the river, out of the water. Farle and Merel began unloading the boat. Anilla stood up and held out her hand to Chris.

'Come on, it's time to meet your new people.'

Chris looked about him, there were a lot of people here. Having no choice in the matter, he took Anilla's hand and, looking around for Bertram, allowed her to lead him off the boat and towards the group who were watching them with interest. Bertram followed close behind. As soon as he could, he reached for Chris, slapping him gently on the back of his shoulder. Chris smiled faintly at him.

'Who we got 'ere then?' Asked the tallest man as they approached.

'This is Chris, and this is Bertram,' Anilla told him, waving a hand at each of them in turn. 'Found them by the Salutem caves, running away I think.' She looked at the boys enquiringly.

'Yeah,' Bertram nodded. 'We were going to get out with our friends, but they got caught. So we thought we'd see for ourselves, so we can go back and tell everyone.'

'But they locked us out.' Chris said in a small voice.

Bertram's arm found its way around Chris' shoulders and he gave him a brief squeeze. Chris was glad of the support, but he was afraid. Afraid of these people, afraid he'd never see his family again, or his friends.

The people of Portum gathered around as news of the newcomers spread. Soon, Chris and Bertram found themselves at the centre of a crowd, with questions being called out, few of which they understood. Fortunately, Anilla was on hand to do a little translating.

'He asks if you like it here?' she said to them, after

one man had shouted the same thing several times.

'Er, well, we've only just got here,' Chris said, taken aback by all the attention. 'I'm finding it all a bit overwhelming to tell you the truth.' Beside him, Bertram nodded in agreement.

Anilla relayed this to the group. Suddenly a woman's voice barked out a command and everyone dispersed, leaving Chris, Bertram, Anilla and a tall woman whose dark hair was arranged in many tiny braids and decorated with beads which glittered in the light.

'This is Narilka,' Anilla said, bowing her head slightly in the woman's direction. 'She's one of our leaders.'

'Oh!' Chris was stunned and shrank back behind Bertram a little.

'Pleased to meet you Narilka.' Bertram said the name slowly and carefully, anxious not to cause offence.

Narilka offered her hand to Bertram, who gripped her forearm without thinking. Narilka looked puzzled for a moment, then gripped his arm in return. A smile played around her lips and she glanced at Anilla.

Chris watched, wide eyed, over Bertram's shoulder. He was aware of Anilla's soft chuckles beside him. When he glanced at her, she was shaking her head, eyes sparkling with amusement.

'Are you hungry?' Narilka's voice was pleasant, now she wasn't yelling at the other folk.

Chris' stomach gurgled just at that moment and he gave a sheepish grin. 'Maybe a little,' he said as everyone laughed, and Bertram nudged him in the ribs.

'Come,' said Narilka. It was an invitation, but it sounded like an order.

They followed Narilka as she headed towards the huts. She led the way to a large, clear area which held a number of tables and benches. This looked more familiar to the boys, it was not unlike the dining hall of Salutem. Smoke rose from a big fire to one side of the area and they caught the smell of food cooking. This time it was Bertram's stomach that betrayed them.

Narilka preceded them and took a seat at one of the tables, indicating to the woman stirring the huge pot hung over the fire that she should serve Chris and Bertram with whatever it was. They were presented with bowls of steaming stew and, as they took their seats at the table, Anilla handed them spoons.

Despite their caution, hunger got the better of Bertram. He lifted a spoonful, gave it a blow, sniffed and began eating. It was good. He lifted his eyes to Narilka. 'This is really good!' he said enthusiastically, before digging in again. To Chris he added, 'It beats Chad's stew! Tuck in!'

Chris lifted a spoonful, tasting slowly before eating with the enthusiasm of one who had last eaten the previous day.

Narilka laughed and passed on Bertram's comments to the woman who had served him. The boys found themselves being handed huge chunks of warm bread to go with their meal. They accepted gratefully and Chris immediately tore off a piece and dunked it into his stew.

When they'd finished the bread and stew, Bertram

sat back with a contented sigh. 'That was lovely. Thank you.'

'You're very welcome.' Narilka smiled at him. Chris noticed she and Anilla had mugs of something in front of them and, just as he wondered what it was, one appeared before him and his bowl was whisked away. He took a cautious sniff before venturing a sip. It was hot and savoury.

'What is this?' he asked.

'We call it Harbatu,' Narilka told him. 'It is an infusion of leaves. Our women have worked on the blend over many years. Do you like it?' She was speaking in the same way Anilla had, so that they could understand her.

Chris nodded and, after giving the brew a blow, he took another sip of the scalding liquid. He glanced at Bertram and grinned, looking around he saw a few other sitting at tables, all had mugs of the Harbatu, a few also had hunks of bread. There was a canvas hut on the edge of the dining area, and beside it were long tables which held piles of plates and tubs full of cutlery. The familiarity comforted him.

'Where do you come from?' Asked Narilka.

'Salutem.' Chris replied. It already felt like a very long time since they'd left, and it had only been that morning. He was about to explain the caves and the people who lived there when Narilka spoke.

'Ah, the old caves near the temple?'

'Temple?' Bertram gave her a querying look. 'I don't know about any temple,' he said. 'Until this morning we'd never been out of the caves.'

'We're not allowed out. They say it's unsafe,' Chris

said, feeling the need to explain.

'Good thing they're wrong then, isn't it?' Narilka laughed again, showing white teeth. 'The last people we took in from there told the same tale.' She shook her head. 'Such a shame.'

Just then a man came over to join them. He was dressed in a similar fashion to Narilka, his dark hair, tied back with some brightly coloured fabric, fell beyond his shoulders. He wore a fur over his right shoulder. He said something to Narilka and then turned to Chris.

'So, you are the young fellows everyone's talking about, are you?'

Chris looked at Bertram who grinned at him, hoping his nerves didn't show. 'We're famous,' he said.

The man laughed, 'I am Fallaren, I am the leader here, Narilka is my mate.' He seated himself next to Chris and raised his hand toward the woman who had brought them their food. A moment later he had a steaming mug of Harbatu in front of him. Raising his mug in salute he took a sip. 'Which of you young men gave Jax the bloody nose?' He asked.

Chris gulped. 'I'm afraid that was me, sir,' he said quietly. He heard quiet chuckles and saw Anilla and Narilka trying not to laugh.

Fallaren laughed. 'I'm not sir to anyone,' he said. 'And it did Jax no harm to be reminded that others may not have the same high opinion of him that he holds himself.'

'Oh.' Chris was shocked to hear the leader of Portum speak this way about someone who must be in a position of trust.

'Jax asked to be leader on that expedition,' Narilka explained, shaking her head at Fallaren. 'It was the first time we'd allowed him to take charge and it went to his head a little. You simply reminded him that, while he's a strong and able hunter, he is also human, just like the rest of us.'

Chris didn't understand everything she said, but her tone was reassuring so he said nothing, simply gave her a small smile and concentrated on his Harbatu.

'How many people live here in Portum? Are there many more like us, who've made it out of Salutem?' Bertram asked, anxious that Chris shouldn't have all the attention.

'A few,' Fallaren nodded. 'From Salutem and other caves. There are plenty of other caves you know, where humans hid themselves away.'

'From the nuclear war,' Bertram said, hoping he sounded knowledgeable.

'No,' Narilka chipped in. 'The Great Dragon war.'

'Pardon?' Chris said, dragging his attention away from his drink. 'Did you say dragon?'

'Oh yes,' Fallaren smiled. 'I suppose you were told they were mythical creatures, were you? Dragons don't exist.' His tone obviously mimicked someone, and Narilka laughed.

Bertram and Chris exchanged looks.

'I don't think they believe us,' Narilka said, nodding towards the silent young men.

Fallaren nodded, 'I think you're right,' he said. 'They're just like the others. Ah well, they will see, all in good time.' he finished his Harbatu and stood up. 'If you'll excuse me, I have much to do. It was good meeting you.' He gave Chris and Bertram a small bow and walked swiftly away.

Bertram looked after him, then turned to Narilka and Anilla. 'What will happen to us now?' he asked.

'Well, you'll be assigned temporary living quarters, of course,' Narilka replied. 'And work duties. Everyone in Portum has a job to do.' A shout echoed across from the river and she turned and stood up abruptly. 'Excuse me, I'll be back shortly. Enjoy your Harbatu. Come Anilla.' The two women left, trotting briskly towards the river.

Bertram turned to Chris, 'Well!' he said with a huff. 'What do you make of all that? I mean, dragons? Really? They must think we're stupid!'

Chris nodded, 'Everyone knows they're not real,' he agreed. 'They're like unicorns and stuff, things little kids believe in.'

He had barely finished speaking when a large, dark shadow moved across them. They both looked up, then, eyes wide, they looked at each other.

'Oh!' was all Chris could say.

'Was that a…a…' Bertram stuttered into silence.

'I think it must be,' Chris said.

The dark shape was turning in the air now and coming back across them. They could see huge wings, a long neck with a wedge-shaped head and a long, arrow-tipped tail.

'Yup, I'd definitely say that's a dragon,' Chris said, his voice was little more than a whisper.

They watched as it swooped across the river to the flat land on the opposite side and landed. Only then did they see the man on its back, sitting at the base of the great neck. He waved cheerily to someone before sliding down from his perch, along a foreleg which the dragon helpfully extended to assist him.

'Didn't that Narilka say there was a great war with the dragons?' Chris said, unable to drag his eyes away from the beast. It was dark green, but its scales sparkled in the sunlight as it arranged its wings across its back and settled down.

'She did,' Bertram nodded. 'Makes you wonder, don't it? I mean, if she's telling us the truth about that, what is a dragon doing here? And with a man on its back? Makes no sense.'

'I know. Maybe they have to tame some of the dragons, you know, to stop them fighting or something?' Chris hazarded.

Bertram shook his head. 'I don't know bro,' he said. 'But surely it can't be safe? If there was a dragon war, then why are they here? Unless they caught some of the beasts like you say,' Bertram murmured. He glanced across at Chris and noted his rapt expression. 'The men who ride those must be heroes,' he said. 'You'd need to be brave indeed to do that, to catch and ride a dragon. They must be revered. Maybe that's how they saved the world?'

Watching the way the dragon rider was greeted by the others, Chris agreed with what Bertram had said. Everyone was warmly welcoming the man and grasping his shoulder or slapping him on the back.

'It looks like you're right,' Chris said. 'He must have such courage.' Although, now he looked more closely at the scene, the dragon didn't seem to pose a threat to anyone, in fact it appeared to be having a nap. 'I want a go on one!' He breathed.

'You? Don't be daft!' Bertram snapped. 'We're newcomers, and besides, you would need to be a senior member of the society here, I'm sure, before they would let you try. I wonder,' he said thoughtfully. 'I wonder how they catch the beasts in order to tame them and train them.' He frowned a little, watching both the rider and the dragon closely, aware that he was fascinated and fearful at the same time. His heart was beating very fast and he had to work hard to control his breathing, he didn't want Chris to think he was afraid.

'Maybe they'd let me have a go,' Chris said, undeterred. 'I'm still not sure I believe what I've just seen, but wouldn't it be a great story to tell when we get back home?'

'Back home?' Bertram's head shot round to look at his friend and former apprentice. 'Bro! You seriously think we'd make it back to Salutem now? Why would you want to? We'd only get thrown into the caves and left to rot, they'd never let us tell folk what we've seen, what we know.'

'But, surely,' Chris began, fear flooding him as he thought of his mother. Of Fen. 'When we got on that boat thing you said you'd remember the way, so we could get back!'

Bertram shook his head. 'I thought it might be possible, but you heard that Jax bloke, no way out of Portum. It'll not happen bro,' he said with a sigh. 'Tolson and his lot would never have us back now anyway, they locked us out, remember?'

'I suppose,' Chris said sadly. He was struggling to keep the tears which were filling his eyes from falling onto his cheeks. He turned away from Bertram, pretending to watch the dragon.

Bertram watched Chris closely, he saw his eyes filling up and dropped his chin to his chest with a huge sigh. 'This was all your idea, you know,' he said.

Startled, Chris turned to him, 'It was all our ideas, I mean you, me, Fen, Baz, Archie, we all decided to escape. Didn't we?' Memories flitted across his mind of how the conversations had gone in the last few days. He dropped his eyes, suddenly fascinated with his mug. 'It was my idea, wasn't it?' he said quietly. 'You guys just went along with it and look where it's got us.'

'Well, it's got us out of those caves and into...this place,' Bertram said, waving his arm to take in as much of Portum as he could, hoping to take the unintended sting out of his words.

'But, what about Fen and the rest?' Chris said. 'I hadn't thought about it, but I'm the reason they're all in the caves now, suffering.'

'No, you're not!' Bertram said sharply. 'If Tolson hadn't put that woman onto us you never would have thought about doing this, not really. Oh, I know we all talked about it, but it was just talk, wasn't it? No, we just reacted to being spied on and followed. We reacted to being fed subliminals, we wanted to choose our own way of life, rather than being kept cooped up in those blasted caves.' Bertram's voice was louder now as he sought to boost Chris out of his maudlin mood.

'But...'

'No!' Bertram almost shouted. 'No more buts Chris. We're here now. Yes, it's all very new to us, and some things are strange and frankly, downright scary.' He glanced at the dragon. 'But it's obvious that these people are a lot happier than we were back in Salutem. I say we should try our best to fit in here, to make a new life for ourselves. We can't go back now; we have to move forwards.'

Chris nodded miserably. He picked up his mug and finished the last of his now cold Harbatu. Perhaps, he thought, they could find a way to get the others out later. He cheered up a little at the thought of showing them their new life, determining to try to do all he could to settle in Portum.

Narilka re-joined them, seating herself next to Chris. 'Is everything all right?' she asked, glancing from Bertram to Chris and back again.

'Yes, thank you, we're fine.' Bertram said abruptly.

'Good, only I thought I heard you arguing a moment ago.'

'Bertram was trying to cheer me up, that's all,' Chris said, unable to raise his eyes to meet the face of either of his companions. 'I realised how different everything is here, and how much I'm missing my family and friends.'

Narilka smiled at him, 'I know things must seem

strange right now,' she said. 'But we will help you adjust, and fairly soon this will all become normal for you. I'm sure you will soon settle in here.' Narilka looked at Bertram. 'Anilla tells me you worked with water machines back in Salutem?' When he nodded, she grinned delightedly, 'Excellent! Our men are developing a method of drawing water from the river. Would you mind lending your expertise to the project?' Her speech had speeded up in her excitement and Bertram frowned as he tried to understand.

'You want me to help them work out how to pump water from the river?' He hazarded.

'Yes,' Narilka nodded. 'Will you?'

'Of course! I'd love to.' It was Bertram's turn to beam delightedly.

'I'll get Anilla to show you where you will be sleeping, you must be tired after your adventurous day. You'll be sharing a hut with a couple of other young men for now. They are newcomers too.' She signalled Anilla as the boys nodded.

'Anilla, please show these boys to their new home. They are exhausted. Tomorrow is soon enough for learning about Portum and what their new life here will entail.' Narilka was smiling but she sounded weary.

'Of course,' Anilla smiled warmly at Bertram and Chris. 'Come with me, we've put you in with Jay and Seb, they came to us a few months ago so they'll understand what you're going through.'

None of this made much sense to them, so they thanked Narilka for her kindness and followed Anilla as she led them across the settlement.

'I'll show you where everything is in the morning,' she told them as they walked. 'You'll soon get to know your way around.'

Chris and Bertram's eyes were darting around, trying to take it all in. The buildings were mostly of similar construction, stones had been used to make the lower walls, up to about waist height. They could see some kind of hard sand holding them together to keep the structure strong. Bertram drew his hand over a wall, nodding his appreciation of the strength. Above the stone wall, the rest of the buildings were made of timber which had been hewn into long slabs. Into the timber were cut large holes and doorways. Curtains fluttered at these openings, all of them in bright colours.

'What's that stuff on the tops?' Chris asked.

Anilla looked puzzled for a moment, until she saw him indicating the roof. 'Ah, that is made of dried grasses,' she told him. 'We gather river reeds, a sort of very rough, very strong grass, and dry them. We've found they make a good, snug roof that keeps the rain off.'

'What's rain?' Bertram asked.

'What? Oh, it's when the sky gets cloudy and droplets of water fall from it.' Anilla looked hopefully at them. Seeing blank expressions, she tried again. 'Clouds,' she pointed to the sky where a few white, fluffy examples could be seen, gold edged against the sky which had deepened from the brilliant blue they'd seen earlier. 'Clouds can get much bigger, and when they do they often drop water, which is called rain.'

'Is it safe?' Chris asked, horrified.

'Yes!' Anilla laughed. 'Perfectly safe, you just get

wet if you're outside when it happens. We protect our homes with the reed roofs to keep everything inside dry, including ourselves.'

'Oh.' Chris wasn't sure he quite understood. Surely dead plants wouldn't be much protection, but he supposed he must accept this as one of the new, strange things he must get used to. 'Where is that sun thing going?' he asked, noticing how it was heading down towards the hills. He was wondering if there was a hole in the hills that would allow the sun to pass through them without problems, or if it would just go out like a candle.

'It's setting,' Anilla said. 'I don't actually know where it goes at night, but it always appears again in the mornings, just over there.' She pointed to the opposite side of Portum. Chris glanced in the direction indicated, confusion written on his face.

'Why is the colour changing?' Bertram asked.

Anilla shrugged. 'I think it's because the sun is setting,' she said. 'As the sun goes down, the light goes with it and the sky changes. Sometimes we have reds and oranges in the sky, it happens in the mornings too, when it rises again. It's very pretty.'

Bertram wasn't sure he thought it was pretty. 'Back home, the lights go out every night at 10pm, unless there's a concert of course.' He said thoughtfully. 'And then they come back on again at 5am. Is the sun like that?'

'Oh. How archaic,' Anilla said. 'We don't have set times for things like that, the sun changes when it gets up and goes down throughout the year. When it gets up earlier, the days are warmer and longer, we call that summer. When it gets up later, the days are shorter and cooler, and we call that winter.'

Chris and Bertram stared at her.

'Back home,' Bertram began. 'It's the same all the time.'

'That's not home anymore, bro.' Chris said quietly.

Bertram sighed. 'I know,' he said, rubbing Chris' upper arm. 'I'm just not sure how many more strange things I can take today. I mean, we're out here, no roof, no walls, it feels...weird. Don't you think?'

Chris nodded. 'Been feeling like that all day bro,' he said. 'It's scary.'

Anilla noted the exchange and hurried them along. They approached a building at the back of the settlement. Here the buildings were smaller and closer together. She pulled aside the curtain which was across the doorway. 'This is where you will be staying for now,' she said.

The house, although small, was remarkably light and airy inside. There were two large openings, from which fluttered bright red and yellow curtains. Against the back wall stood a set of bunk beds, another set stood against the right-hand wall. There were two beds to a set, each bed was made neatly and covered with brightly coloured blankets. On the left was a table with four chairs tucked underneath it and to the right, at the end of the beds, stood a large cupboard. The floor was freshly swept and covered with bright rugs and the overall effect was homely.

'This is really nice!' Chris said, stepping right into the hut and looking around him. 'Feels good to have walls and a roof over my head!'

Anilla stood by the door, watching with a smile on her face.

'Who else did you say we will be sharing with?' Bertram asked, indicating the bunks.

'A couple of the boys stay here. Jay and Seb are brothers,' Anilla said. 'Don't worry, they're really friendly. They came to us from another cave community, a little East of Salutem.'

Chris was nodding as she spoke. 'That sounds good,' he said. 'They'll understand how we feel.'

'Does everyone eat at that place where we had the stew?' Bertram asked.

'The dining area? Usually, yes,' Anilla said. 'A few prefer to eat privately in their homes sometimes, but it's normal for most of us gather and eat together.'

This was a new concept to Chris and Bertram. In their former home there were no facilities for privacy of any kind. 'Nice that there are options here,' Bertram said softly. Chris nodded.

Just then a boy entered the room, he leaned against the door frame, panting. His hair was long and dark curls were escaping from the string he had used to tie it back from his face. His face was tanned but his nose was bright red and peeling. The sleeves on his tunic had ridden up to reveal very white arms beneath. He nodded at Anilla and brown eyes looked curiously at Chris and Bertram.

'Ah, Jay,' she said. 'This is Bertram, and Chris, your new roommates.'

'Hi,' Jay nodded at them. 'Seb told me we had new

folks.'

'Hello,' Bertram decided to be bold, he held out his hand, which Jay gripped firmly.

'You'll soon get settled in,' Anilla said. 'Jay has been here for a while now, I'm sure he and Seb will show you around and help you, just as they were helped when they arrived here.' She looked meaningfully at Jay as she spoke.

'Of course.' Jay stood up straighter. 'I was asked to come and find the one who knows about pumps, we're gonna need all the help we can get out there.'

'That's me.' Bertram said. 'Although Chris worked with me, so he understands too.'

'Nah, they told me you were the one. Bertram?' Jay said his name slowly and clearly. 'They tell me you're from Salutem, is that right?'

'Yeah, just got out.' Bertram laughed. 'I make it sound like prison.'

Jay laughed. 'Well, you'll be working with me out in the bright sunshine for now,' he said. 'You're gonna love it here. Although perhaps not the sunshine so much, at least at the start, till your skin gets used to it.' He rubbed his red nose gently.

'Well, if you used the ointment we gave you, you wouldn't have so many issues!' Anilla sounded frustrated. Jay grinned cheekily at her.

Chris yawned so much his jaw cracked making Anilla jump. 'You need to go to bed,' she said. 'Jay, can you show him where the necessaries are please, then let them sleep.' Turning to the newcomers she smiled. 'I'll see you in the morning for breakfast, then I can show you around properly.'

They bid her goodnight and in a very short while they were both tucked up in their bunks. Seb appeared soon after, almost a carbon copy of his brother. He barely said hello to them. He washed, fell into his bed and was asleep very soon afterwards.

Chris had thought that he would be asleep as soon as his head touched the pillow, but the day had been so full of strangeness that he couldn't sleep. There were curious noises. He could hear the river, he could hear other people moving about, and, in the distance, a roar. Then a light appeared outside, bright and silvery. After the near complete silence and darkness of Salutem, he found it all too much. He tossed and turned for a while before deciding to get up and go outside to see what the noises were, and what the strange, pale light was.

He slipped from his bed and walked silently to the doorway. Pulling aside the curtain he stepped out into a different world. Looking up he saw a new light in the inky black sky, this one milky white and glowing, giving the settlement a strange, shadowy appearance. Around it were lots of small, twinkling lights. Chris thought it was very pretty. He made his mind up to ask Anilla about it in the morning.

He didn't know how long he stood there, gazing about him, but he was suddenly aware of being cold. Shivering, he went back inside and climbed gratefully into his bed, snuggling under the covers.

Chapter 4 - Beginnings

The following morning, they went with Jay and Seb to get breakfast. The area where they had eaten yesterday was now packed with people. Chris hung back and drew closer to Bertram.

'This is like being back in Salutem,' he murmured. 'Except here we don't know anyone.'

Jay noticed Chris' reluctance. 'C'mon, I'll show you what to do. It's a bit much at first, isn't it?'

Chris, grateful for Jay's friendly approach, allowed himself to be steered towards a long table laden with dishes. While Jay and Seb quickly served themselves with food, Chris and Bertram looked at the spread suspiciously.

'What is this?' Bertram asked, spooning something brown from its dish and letting it drain back in. He sniffed experimentally before putting the serving spoon back.

'Dunno,' Chris said, looking up and down the table hoping for something familiar. 'Look, there's some bread at least,' he said, pointing to the end of the table. As he was reaching for it, a woman approached them with a platter of bacon and sausages. Chris looked questioningly at her before reaching tentatively for a sausage. The woman said something he didn't understand, but it sounded like he was being scolded, so he dropped the sausage quickly and picked up more bread. She stopped him, held his wrist, and smiled.

'You need more food,' she said slowly, heaping sausages and several rashers of bacon onto his plate.

Chris stared wide eyed. 'Thank you,' he stammered watching helplessly as she put a couple of fried eggs on there too. Then, with a wave of her hand, he was dismissed. Chris glanced to his side and saw Bertram's plate was similarly loaded.

Bertram was looking around at the busy tables, eventually spotting Jay and Seb. 'This way, the others are over there.' He began to lead the way, weaving between the crowded tables. 'Certainly eat well here, don't they,' he said over his shoulder. Chris, already chewing a sausage, could only nod in agreement.

Seb looked up as they reached the table and waved his spoon to indicate they should sit and eat. 'You like?' he asked between mouthfuls.

'Yeah!' Chris breathed. 'We were never allowed to eat as much as we liked in Salutem, we were given rations. Breakfast was already on plates for us. It saves time and arguments.' He put on a pompous voice and beside him Bertram spluttered at the accurate impression of the man in charge of the dining hall.

'It was the same where we're from too,' Jay told them. 'Just about enough to eat, but some of it was... different!' He returned his attention to his breakfast, spearing his third sausage and dunking it into his egg yolk.

'You'll need this,' Seb said, indicating their food. 'We work hard here, but they look after us all really well. We found being outside made us even hungrier at first, but no one said anything when we ate like dragons.'

Chris glanced at Bertram to see if he'd caught the

67

mention of dragons, but he was busy with his food. Chris had never seen him enjoy his breakfast so much.

Jay finished and pushed his plate away from him with a sigh. 'That was lovely!' he announced. 'Proper set me up for the day that has.' He grinned at Bertram. 'When you're ready I'll take you to old Bashta, he's in charge of the pipe idea.'

'I'm starting today?' Bertram asked. 'I thought we were being given a tour of the place by that Anilla woman.'

Jay shrugged. 'It's unusual,' he said. 'But I was told to take you with me. They're desperate for folk who know what they're doing with this kind of thing. I'm sure you'll get the chance to look round later.'

Bertram nodded, mopping up the last of his egg with a scrap of bread. 'Ready when you are then,' he said, still chewing his last mouthful.

Seb laughed. 'Drink your batu first,' he said. 'There's no rush.'

Bertram noticed a mug of the drink they had been served the previous day had appeared next to him. 'Where'd that come from?'

'They like to make sure you get a drink with your meal, everyone's the same here.' Seb explained. 'You didn't pick one up, so Scoria brought you both one over.'

'Where do you work Seb?' Chris asked.

'I'm training with the healers,' Seb replied. 'It's what I was doing back home...in Barlang...' he inclined his head to Jay, who had drawn breath to chastise his brother. 'I got here, told them what I was good at and they put me straight into the hospital.'

'Hospital?' Bertram looked confused.

'It's just what they call the place where the healers work. If anyone's ill or injured they get taken there, keeps it all in one place, nice and tidy like.'

Chris and Bertram nodded, another new word for them to learn.

Bertram finished his drink and looked expectantly at Jay, who put his mug down at the same moment.

'Right? Ready for work Bertie?' Jay said. Bertram winced and nodded. Jay produced a couple of cloth hats and handed one to Bertram. 'Best wear these, or I'll be in trouble for not looking after you.'

Bertram put his hat on, it was a tighter fit than the one Anilla had woven for them the previous day. There was a stiff peak at the front to shield the eyes and a long flap at the back which covered his neck. He turned to Chris, who was snorting with laughter. 'No use asking what you think.' Bertram huffed.

Jay put on his own hat. 'You'll be grateful for this,' he said. 'Saves a lot of pain. Right, off we go. See ya laters lads.'

'I have to go too,' Seb said to Chris, standing up and stacking all their plates together. 'If I take these back, can you bring the mugs when you're done? They all go over there.' He pointed to a fabric hut where a table was stacked high with dishes. Chris nodded mutely.

Then he was alone.

He took his time finishing his Harbatu, wondering what he was supposed to do now. He had no work assigned to him; he had no idea where anything was. He sighed, missing his family and the safety and routine of Salutem more than ever.

Just as he was gathering the mugs together to take them to the cleaning station, someone slapped him on the back. He turned and found Anilla standing behind him. His eyes widened as he took in her changed appearance. Gone were the green robes and wild hair of the previous day. She wore a simple sleeveless top and trousers. A belt around her waist held a pouch. Her hair had been tamed into a long braid.

'Ready for your guided tour?' Anilla asked cheerfully, then she noticed how unhappy he looked. 'Are you alright?'

'I'm fine,' Chris said. 'I was thinking about my family and friends.' Anilla gave him a sad little smile. 'And I felt a bit lost after everyone went to work,' he continued. 'Never been on my own before.'

'I'd heard it was like that in the caves,' Anilla said. 'Not enough room I suppose.'

Chris shook his head, 'I grew up knowing no different,' he said. 'Now I'm here and it's scary. Out in the open, no routine, alone.' He lowered his head, trying to suppress a shudder.

'You'll be fine you know,' Anilla said quietly. 'We'll get you sorted. Get a bit of colour to your skin and some muscles built up and you'll not look back.' She was smiling confidently now. 'Jay and Seb were just the same when they came to us. Pale, weedy, scared of their own shadows. Now look at them!'

'I suppose.' Chris wasn't convinced, but he was here

now, he had no choice. He squared his shoulders and lifted his chin. 'What about this tour then?'

'Atta boy!' Anilla said, clearly delighted, 'We'll just take these back, then we'll set off, hope you had a good breakfast.'

'Oh yes!' Chris patted his stomach and his smile was genuine. 'It was lovely, never eaten so well.'

'Brilliant! You'll need that, lots of walking for you today.'

They strolled across to the cleaning station, which Anilla called a tent, and she chatted for a few moments to the women there, while Chris attempted to stack the mugs neatly so they wouldn't fall over.

'Ready?' Anilla looked at him.

'What were you saying to them?' he asked as soon as they were out of earshot. 'You were speaking so quickly I couldn't understand.'

Anilla's face split in a grin. 'I was saying how you loved your food, that you told me you'd never eaten so well. You'll get looked after especially well from now on, they like to see a healthy appetite. And telling them their food's good is never a bad idea.'

Chris laughed, stopping abruptly as Anilla handed him a hat similar to the one Jay had made Bertram wear. He looked at it dubiously before putting it on with a sigh.

'We'd better get on or we'll never get through everything. The large buildings here,' Anilla said, indicating a series of long, low buildings set around an open area. 'Are the communal buildings, those are where the leaders meet, where we have our big celebrations, the bath house and so on.'

Chris gazed at the stone walls. They all looked the same to him, would he ever know his way around?

Several chickens appeared round the corner of one building, pursued by a gaggle of children who were attempting to herd the birds. Anilla stepped aside. 'Escapees,' she said. 'A little like you.'

'You have farming here?' Chris asked, watching the chase. One of the chickens was captured, squawking, and flapping in protest. It was quickly subdued and carried carefully back the way it had come by a young boy who was crooning softly to the bird as he passed Chris and Anilla.

'Of course! We're not savages,' Anilla said. 'The farms are on the outer edges of the settlement; you'll see them in a while. The fencing usually keeps the animals out of the streets.'

'Streets?'

'This,' Anilla swept her arm forwards and backwards to indicate the path they had taken. 'We call this a street. The gaps between rows of buildings I suppose.' Chris took in the street. Grass wasn't growing much here, instead there was sand and fine grit, which had been trodden into hard paths. Here and there, clumps of grass were hanging on, and among these, flowers bloomed, giving bright splashes of yellow, pink and purple.

'So you fence the farms in?'

'Yes, we need to keep the animals in their fields or they cause havoc. You can see the fence if you look down here.' She indicated a long straight street which led to the edge of the settlement. After the buildings there was a grassy space, then a wooden fence. On the other side of the fence the cattle peacefully munched the grass.

'We have animals in Salutem too,' Chris said. 'But not like this. There are chickens, pigs and a few sheep too, we use the wool.'

Anilla nodded. 'We have sheep,' she said. 'I'm not sure where the farmers have them at the moment. Our lands here are quite vast you know, we use all of this basin. It gives us a good life.'

'Anilla,' Chris blurted suddenly as they walked along the street, heading out of the main settlement. 'Can you tell me about the dragons please. What happened with the war? Why are dragons here with people if they're so dangerous? How do they catch them and tame them?'

Anilla frowned, 'You really don't know about the war?' she asked. 'Well, no, obviously you don't. The great dragon war,' she continued with a sigh, 'was many years ago, generations ago. Wild dragons began hunting humans,'

'Hunting? To eat?' Chris squeaked.

'Yes, unfortunately.' Anilla said sadly. 'That is why so many communities abandoned their cities and made lives for themselves underground. There are many cave systems which hold populations you know. Portum itself was originally a cave settlement.'

'Really?'

'Yes, the people lived in the caves the dragons use now, but some of them had the idea that dragons weren't all bad. They wanted to try domesticating them, like dogs.'

'Big dogs!' Chris said, half laughing.

Anilla nodded. 'I know it sounds improbable, but they did it. The story goes that someone found a clutch of eggs which they thought had been abandoned. They brought the eggs to the caves here for safety until they hatched. Then allowed people to interact with the baby dragons, to see if they could be taught to be loyal to humans rather than see us as prey. They discovered that each dragon imprinted on a human and developed strong bonds.'

'Wow,' Chris breathed. 'They were brave. What if the eggs hadn't been abandoned at all, what if the dragon had caught them?'

'I know! The story has been handed down and it's probably changed over time, but that is the story of how we came to be guardians of the dragons. Well, some of the dragons, there is still a large wild population and they don't like our tame dragons much. We do have issues with them, and our riders must be battle trained, for the protection of us and our dragons. It's quite a responsibility.'

Chris listened; eyes wide. 'The riders must be like heroes.' He grinned as a thought struck him. 'Back in Salutem we have a rock band named The Flaming Heroes!'

Anilla laughed. 'Appropriate! Yes our riders are held in high regard.'

'So, do you still steal eggs?'

'No, our dragons lay all the eggs we can cope with,' Anilla said. 'We have a clutch now. I can show you. Would you like that?' Chris nodded eagerly, so she changed direction, heading towards the farthest hills, right at the back of the basin.

They walked for a long time, passing fields of cattle and a field which held several small stone buildings around which pigs were lazing in the sunshine. Chris saw crops growing, a farmer was walking among the tall, golden stalks, inspecting the seed heads. Finally, they reached the hills. As they drew nearer, they entered a narrow valley and Chris could see beyond the grassy hills to the sheer rock faces beyond, which were dotted with cave entrances. Gaping black holes in the otherwise smooth stone wall. Some of the caves sported sunbathing dragons, their scales glittering in the bright light.

Mesmerised, stumbling over rocks as the path grew rougher, Chris could see a huge lake to the right, and several folk going about their business. A man with a handcart loaded with vegetables was shouting at someone Chris couldn't see, and at the water's edge some women were washing clothes. He could hear their shrill laughter as they worked.

'Not far now.' Anilla said, pointing to a huge cave opening at ground level on their right. The river was narrow here and ran over gravel, with great plumes of tall grasses here and there. 'We need to paddle for this bit,' she told him, stepping out into the shallow water, her booted feet crunching the gravel. Chris followed suit, trudging unsteadily as the gravel shifted beneath his weight.

His heart was beating fast as they entered the enormous cave. It was cool in here, and damp. It was comforting to have rock around him and the darkness was a relief after the brilliant sunshine, but Chris couldn't help thinking they needed the systems which were in place in Salutem. Their caves were always dry and warm. As they walked further in and rounded a corner, he saw the dragon. It was curled up and looked to be sleeping. Next to it was a clutch of mottled eggs, a couple of them were almost as big as he was. He stopped in his tracks and simply stared.

'Come on,' Anilla urged him.

'Won't the dragon...' Chris whispered. 'Won't the dragon wake up and chase us, or something?' Thanks to their earlier conversation he could imagine far worse things a dragon could do to a person. He gulped.

'No, silly,' said Anilla. 'This is Taivas. She is one of our dragons. Her rider is my sister, Saff. She's perfectly safe.'

Chris gawped at her. 'Your sister is a rider of dragons?' His voice was barely a whisper. 'Girls can do that?'

'Well, obviously,' Anilla was laughing at him now. 'Are girls not treated equally to boys where you come from?'

Chris thought about Fen and his heart gave a little lurch. 'No,' he said quietly. 'A friend of mine wants to train to be a healer but they won't give her promotion, or proper training, because she's female. Yet a lad who is younger than her was put straight into the programme. She was very annoyed about that. She's stuck cleaning up, scrubbing floors, washing...things.' His voice faltered a little, it felt strange talking about it, like Salutem was a lifetime ago.

'I bet she was annoyed!' Anilla's voice was heated.

'Does she have talent? Do you think she would be a good healer?'

Chris nodded. 'Yes, she's very good. Not always as calm as she could be, but when they treat her like that...'

'Who can blame her,' Anilla finished. 'Shame she didn't make it out with you and Bert,' she continued. 'It sounds like she could have done well here.'

Chris noted the shortening of his friend's name, the second time this morning, but couldn't take his eyes off Taivas. 'She would love it here,' he said slowly. 'Anilla, how do they choose who will ride the dragons? How does it work?'

"The leaders make those decisions, and they give basic training to anyone chosen,' she told him. 'Then, when the eggs are ready to hatch the dragons all make this weird warbling noise, and everyone comes to the cave. Those who have been selected stand close to the eggs and wait. When the eggs hatch the baby dragons choose who they want. It's wonderful to watch. I saw Saff being paired with Taivas here.' Her eyes were shining as she recalled the event.

'So how are you selected?' Chris asked.

'The leaders watch us,' she said. 'They know who is capable of handling all that bonding with a dragon entails. It's a lot of hard work. Why? Thinking of giving it a try?' Chris was studying his own boots, his cheeks bright pink. 'You might make it one day, but I'd focus on getting settled in here first if I were you. You're just out of Salutem, you need to get used to living here and how we do things first.' Anilla laughed.

Taivas opened an eye.

Chris was mesmerised, staring at the huge eye that whirled in rainbow hues as it focused on him and Anilla. Then the beast shifted and stood, taking a few steps towards them. Chris scuttled behind Anilla, who laughed at him and held up a hand to the dragon. Taivas' tongue flickered as she took in Anilla's scent and that of the young man hiding behind her. Then her head snaked out on its long, sinewy neck and swivelled to look directly at him.

Chris, terrified, drew closer to Anilla. 'What's... what's it doing?'

'It is she, and she is finding out about you and saying hello.' Anilla said quite briskly. 'I have to say Chris, this is not the behaviour of someone who wants to be a rider.'

Taivas was still taking an interest in him, so Anilla stepped smartly aside leaving Chris exposed. He felt himself trembling as the dragon dropped her head until her chin was almost on the floor in front of him, her eyes level with his. He could feel her warm breath, whistling round his ankles, and see her scales gleaming dully silver and gold. The dragon regarded him calmly for a while, then nudged him with her nose.

'She wants you to stroke her,' Anilla said.

Chris turned terrified eyes to her. 'Stroke her?'

'Yes,' Anilla nodded. 'Go on, she won't hurt you.'

Tentatively, Chris raised his hand and stroked the dragon's nose. It was softer than he had imagined. He ran his hand upwards along the middle of her face, he had expected the scales to be quite rough, but her skin was silky smooth and cool. Quite suddenly, the dragon raised her head and trundled back to the eggs, tongue flickering protectively over them. Then she settled down again, wrapping her long tail around her clutch.

'What was all that about?' Chris breathed.

'I think she likes you,' Anilla said. 'Come on, we should probably go now.'

'I touched a dragon!' Chris wore an expression of wide-eyed wonder as he continued to stare at Taivas. 'I actually touched an actual dragon.'

Reluctantly, he allowed Anilla to take hold of his arm and pull him away. They turned and retraced their steps out of the cave and back into the bright sunlight.

'How long will it be until the eggs hatch?' he asked, squinting as they emerged and adjusting the brim of his hat.

'Taivas only laid them in the last day or two, so we're going to have to wait for a couple of months. Then you'll get to see your first hatching, it's very exciting.' Anilla smiled happily.

'Are you hoping to get a dragon?'

'It would be lovely, but they are hard work, and it means you have less time for other tasks. They're not pets you know, caring for a baby dragon is hard work, not to mention all the training we do with them. Although, flying to other settlements with messages must be fun.'

'Other settlements?' Chris looked stunned. His world had expanded so much today that he couldn't take it in.

'Yes, there are several quite nearby,' Anilla said. 'And in the whole world? Oh there must be thousands of people still living above ground. Most of them have at least a couple of dragons living with them.'

Chris was shaking his head. 'The day before yesterday, I thought Salutem was the world,' he said slowly. 'Then Bertram and I got outside and found the trees and river and the...' he faltered, not knowing the words. 'Big, flat green places.'

'Grasslands, or plains,' Anilla supplied.

'Grasslands,' Chris repeated. 'Then we were brought here and suddenly there are lots of things to learn and there's no roof and there are dragons. And now you tell me there are even more places?' He put a hand to his head and closed his eyes.

***

As they entered the main settlement a loud bell rang. Suddenly the quiet street was filled with people, all of them seemed to be heading towards the river.

'Lunch time,' Anilla told him in response to the startled look he gave her.

'Have we been all morning? That went fast!'

'We have indeed,' Anilla smiled. 'Think you can find your way on your own? I have a couple of things I need to do.'

Chris nodded uncertainly. 'I think so.'

'Good, I'll see you later then.' And she was gone, weaving between people and buildings.

Chris turned and headed in the same direction as everyone else and in a couple of minutes he was joining the queue for lunch. He was serving himself with stew and fresh bread when someone tapped him on the shoulder. He turned to see Bertram grinning at him.

'Don't forget your batu,' he said, pointing to the steaming mugs. 'Then come sit with us, we're over there.' He pointed to a table a few rows back, then went back to his lunch.

Chris picked up a mug and made his way carefully to the table where Bertram, Jay and another boy he didn't know were sitting. He took the empty seat and sat with a sigh. He hadn't realised how hungry and tired he was.

'Chris, this is Sam,' Bertram introduced the new man with a casual wave of a hand. Sam nodded at Chris before continuing with his conversation with Jay.

Chris nodded in return and began his attack on his meal. 'Can't believe how hungry I am after that huge breakfast,' he said to Bertram through a mouthful of stew.

'I know right? But apparently it's normal. Jay says he and Seb were the same for the first few weeks. What you been doing this morning?'

Chris told him of his morning with Anilla. Bertram was suitably impressed with his tale of the dragon and her eggs.

'Wish I'd been there.' Bertram said, before telling of his morning with Bashta, Sam and Jay. He was baffling Chris with the language he was using, talking about hydro electrics. Chris nodded and ate, his mind still swimming with thoughts of Taivas.

'What work have you been assigned to?' Jay asked him.

'I dunno,' Chris shrugged, pulling himself back

into the present. 'Nothing's been mentioned yet.'

'Fair enough,' Jay said good naturedly. 'They'll let you settle first, I guess. Bertie was put to work faster than normal cos of his skills with the water systems.'

Bertram chose to ignore the nickname, instead preening a little. 'I was shift manager back in Salutem, wasn't I?'

'Yeah,' Chris said. 'He was my supervisor; he was training me.'

While the others all chatted about what they were to do that afternoon, Chris sat quietly, contemplating his future. Obviously Bertram was happy with the way things were looking for him, no doubt heading for a position of authority again. Chris wondered sadly what would happen to him. He lacked Bertram's skills and confidence. He sighed, was he destined to be the apprentice, again?

***

After they had eaten, and the others headed back to work, Anilla appeared at his side.

'Ready for the rest of your guided tour?' she asked him.

'Yeah, sure,' he said, pushing himself up and starting to gather his dishes together. 'What work do you think I'll be doing here?' he asked as they made their way to the tent to drop off the used dishes.

Anilla looked surprised. 'I don't know,' she said. 'I'm sure someone will be having a chat with you soon, about your skills and so on. We lost so many of the old skills you know, when people were forced to flee during the war.' She sighed, 'But you'll not be forced into doing something you don't want to, you know.'

Chris nodded. 'I was just wondering,' he said in a small voice. 'With Bertram looking like he's settled into his job already.'

'That's very unusual,' Anilla told him. 'And it's only a temporary thing. Relax, they'll get you put to work soon enough, enjoy this quiet time while you can.'

That afternoon she took him right around the settlement, showing him the weaving sheds, stacked with bales of wool, and huge looms banging back and forth. In the far corner, some women sat with strange contraptions, pedalling with their feet to spin wheels. They had piles of fleece beside them.

'What are they doing?' Chris asked, pointing to the women.

'Spinning,' Anilla replied, as if that answered everything. Seeing his curious look, she continued. 'They are turning the fleeces into wool, a thick thread, that can be woven into cloth or knitted into jumpers and so on.'

Chris smiled as the penny dropped. 'My Mother used to tell me about that, back home...in Salutem,' he corrected. 'I never saw it before though.'

Their next visit was to the farms. One of the senior farmers showed him the fields of crops for food, the medicinal plants, the fields of cotton and hemp for making fibres for weaving. Then they went into the dairy, a large, cool room where cheese and butter were made.

Back in the barns he saw animals being cared for. A healer who specialised in animals was in a pen with a pig. As Chris watched, the healer stabbed a vicious looking thorn into the animal and squeezed the tube connected to the thorn. The pig squealed but, as soon as it tried to move away the healer whisked the thorn out and gave it a good slap. The pig shook its head and trotted away from him towards its feed trough, all thoughts of the thorn forgotten.

'Why do they do that?' Chris asked the farmer.

'He's giving it medicine,' came the gruff reply. 'Looks terrible don't it? They soon forgets though.'

Watching the pig snuffling in the feed, Chris had to agree.

They visited the wood carving workshops which smelled fresh and earthy. He saw apprentices using tools to strip thin slices of wood away, creating white piles by their feet as table legs appeared beneath their hands.

Anilla showed him the hospital, with its clean smelling rooms and corridors. He saw Seb briefly, who waved and smiled at him. Outside, he saw the gardens where medicinal herbs were grown, then Anilla took him into the wing of the hospital which housed the laboratories. He saw, from a safe distance, herbs being dried, treated and ground up. Huge copper vats were steaming and pipes were hissing. Glass flasks collected the drips.

'This is called the distillery,' Anilla said, waving at a collection of pipes and vats, one of which had a fire burning beneath it. 'They're making medicines.'

'It pongs a bit,' said Chris, holding his nose, his eyes watering.

Anilla laughed and ushered him back outside to the gardens. Bees buzzed among the flowering herbs and he saw a strangely shaped little hut in the corner.

'It's a beehive,' Anilla told him. 'Where the bees live. They pollinate the plants and they give us honey and wax.' She said this with happy satisfaction. Chris didn't understand a word of it, but he nodded and hoped she wouldn't be asking him questions later.

'What is your job?' he asked her.

'I look after the bees,' she told him. 'And I help gather the herbs, here and over at the farm too. When we found you, we were returning from a trip gathering wild herbs.'

'Are you sure you have time to be showing me round?'

'Of course,' she said. 'I'm happy to be doing this, I like making sure newcomers are well settled with us.'

Next on the tour was the brewery. It was hot and steamy with a tang of strange spiciness. The brewers were cheerful folk in heavy leather aprons. They showed him the fields where they grew hops and grapes, the presses where the juice was squeezed from the grapes, the big vats of beers in various stages of brewing. One man was skimming froth from the top of a vat and putting it into a bucket.

'What's he doing?' Chris asked the brewer who was showing them around.

'He's taking the yeast off the top,' the man explained. 'We send most of it down to the kitchens for bread making.'

'Yeast makes bread rise; it makes it light and fluffy.' Anilla told him.

'Smells nice,' Chris said, taking deep, appreciative breaths. 'Much better than the hospital laboratories,' he grinned, taking his time over the strange new words.

'Where you off to next?' the brewer asked Anilla.

'To the tanners,' she said. 'Speaking of strange smells.'

The brewer laughed and waved as they left him.

'What do you mean about strange smells?' Chris asked her warily.

'You'll see,' Anilla said. 'Just don't go taking any deep breaths when we get to the tannery, you'll regret it if you do.'

Bewildered, Chris followed her along the hard, sandy path to the tannery, which was right at the back of the settlement, away from all the other buildings. Large, wide doors were open in the front and he could see men hauling tubs on wheels between frames on which animal skins were stretched.

Anilla took him inside and he immediately understood her warning. The place reeked! Catching his expression, Anilla grinned and gestured towards a door in the far corner. Chris hurried towards it, Anilla right behind him.

Through the door was another world. Here men worked at long, sturdy benches cutting leather and sewing it into harnesses and clothing. Over in the corner two men were making shoes. There was cheerful chatter here, along with an air of quiet industry. One of the men looked up.

'Just bringing our latest recruit for a look around,'

Anilla said. The man nodded to them and returned his attention to his work.

Their next stop was the river. Together they crossed the water on a floating platform held in place by a system of ropes and pulleys, and then they walked across the grassy land in the middle of the two river channels, past a series of wooden huts with strangely shaped, woven pots stacked outside. A couple of older men were sitting on stools making nets. They walked towards the deeper part of the river. Here were fishermen with nets and rods, and women gathering bunches of tall grasses that Anilla told him were reeds. The men showed Chris where they farmed some of the fish. Chris was given a small bag of food to throw into one of the pools. He did so and was startled as the water came alive with fish splashing and fighting for the food.

A little further along another huge shed was busy with men making a large boat. They were singing as they worked, a lilting tune which blended all their voices together in harmony. Chris was proud he remembered the Oword for what they were making. This was a flat-bottomed boat, similar to the one Anilla and the others had been using when they found him and Bertram. He sniffed appreciatively at the clean, woody smell, giving Anilla a cheeky grin as he did so.

'Where next?' Chris asked as they left the boat builders.

'Well now, let's see,' Anilla paused. 'We have the miners, but I don't want to take you over there, it's dangerous and, to be honest, I don't think it would suit you.'

'Miners?' Chris looked quizzically at her. 'I'm sure

we heard bangs and noises from over there when we arrived.'

'Yes, they use explosives sometimes, that's what makes the noises, er,' Anilla struggled for words he would understand. 'Explosives, things that make loud bangs and clear lots of rocks away quickly.' She saw his confusion. 'They dig?' She looked at him for confirmation he understood. When he nodded she continued. 'They dig under the ground, deep underground, and find coal...soft black rocks we use for fires...and metal ores and gems, like the ones you saw Narilka and Fallaren wearing.'

Chris nodded, remembering the leaders and especially Narilka's hands with their rings.

'Then there's the smiths,' Anilla continued. 'They do things to the ores and gems,' she sounded uncertain now. 'I'm not sure what they do, but it's usually quite loud and it's very hot in there.' She pointed to a row of buildings near the mine.

'And what's that place?' he asked, pointing to a smaller building farther down on the other side of the river.

'That's where they make paper and books.' Anilla told him.

Chris was curious. 'Make paper? I didn't know it was possible,' he said.

'We only have a couple of people who know how to do it,' Anilla explained. 'So paper and books are really quite unusual.'

'Can we go see?' Chris asked, his interest roused.

'Sure,' Anilla shrugged. 'Don't see why not, and Fallaren did say he wanted you to see everything, so they can't complain can they?'

Wondering why the paper makers would complain about receiving visitors, Chris went with her towards the walkway that crossed this section of the river. Anilla told him it was called a bridge. It was sturdily built, with a couple of stone steps up to the narrow walkway which had a handrail on one side. There were stone steps at the opposite side and Chris jumped down these, Portum on the path, which led in two directions. One led to the mines, the other to the papermaker's building, which sat close by the river on the highest part of the bank. Anilla knocked on the door, the first time she had done so in their whole tour, before opening it and walking in.

'Hey! What do you think you're doing? Out!' shouted a gruff, deep voice.

'Bringing our newest lad on a tour. Fallaren's orders,' Anilla replied, standing a little straighter.

Chris entered the building behind her and stood for a moment, looking around. There were wooden frames full of soggy mush, some strange looking equipment and, at the end of the room, a man was sitting at a bench sewing sheets of paper together, while another prepared what Chris thought would be the cover of a book. Suddenly he was fascinated.

'What's that?' he asked, pointing to the mushed-up stuff in the frames.

'What's it to do with you?' grumbled the older man. His hair and beard were grizzled and grey and there were heavy wrinkles around his eyes.

'He's just interested,' Anilla snapped. 'No work specialism has been assigned to him yet, and unless I'm much mistaken you two have been moaning for months about your workload and not getting any help. You might find yourselves with an apprentice if you don't scare him off with your grumbling.'

'Humph.' The man stood up, easing his back, and walked slowly towards Chris, taking a good look at the young man before him. Chris raised his chin and tried to look confident. The man was apparently satisfied. 'This is wood pulp,' he gestured to the trays. 'We soak it like this, then press it into sheets to make the paper. It takes a while and it's fiddly work.'

'But you're making paper,' Chris said quietly. 'Actual paper, and books!' He couldn't help being impressed, back in Salutem there had been some books, but they had to be handled very carefully and only important people had been allowed to touch them.

'Interested, are you?' This time it was the younger man who spoke.

Chris surprised himself by nodding. 'I am,' he said. 'I never realised you could do this, it's brilliant!' He smiled the biggest smile Anilla had seen from him.

'I'll make sure I tell Fallaren,' she said. The men nodded, looking at Chris curiously.

'Where you from lad?' asked the older man.

'Salutem,' Chris said.

The men exchanged glances.

As they left and the door shut behind them, Chris heard the men talking, their deep voices were indistinguishable but Anilla looked pleased.

'That gave the miserable pair something to think about,' she said with satisfaction. 'Now, I think we're almost done, which is a good thing as the sun's setting. Only one place left to go, might have to wait till morning. Come on, let's head back.'

***

It wasn't until they neared the main settlement that Chris realised how tired he felt. His legs were heavy and he struggled to keep up with Anilla. She turned and saw him drooping. 'Soon be dinner time,' she said. 'Why don't we go and get seats now? Then, after you've eaten, I think you'll be in for a treat.'

Chris was confused, and certain he wanted nothing more than to fall into bed, but he obediently followed her to the eating area, slumping down onto the nearest bench and leaning his head onto his arms with a groan. It had been a very long, tiring day. The back of his neck was burning, despite the hat he still wore and his arms were bright red.

It wasn't long before he heard lots of voices approaching. The bench rocked as Bertram, Jay and Seb sat down at the table with him, along with a couple of others Chris didn't recognise.

'Alright bro?' Bertram asked, nudging him with an elbow. 'Good day?'

'Yeah,' Chris nodded, forcing himself to sit up straighter and trying not to yawn. 'It was interesting.'

'Good!' Bertram was in sparkling form this evening. 'You didn't mind, you know, not having walls and a roof then?' Bertram was grinning now, in a not altogether friendly manner. Chris noticed his friend's face was red, so were his arms.

'No, I was fine,' Chris said rather more firmly than he'd meant to, trying to forget the odd bouts of panic he'd experienced during the day. 'Having the hat helped.' He tapped the brim, still firmly placed above his eyes. 'How 'bout you?'

Jay was watching the exchange. 'Bertie had a couple of moments,' he said before Bertram could deny it. Bertram looked annoyed. 'And the sun caught him. You too mate,' he indicated Chris' red arms. 'Need to sort 'em out tonight Seb. Decided what you want to do yet?' Jay asked Chris, ignoring the look Bertram was throwing at him.

'Maybe,' Chris said. 'Not sure if I'll be allowed though, don't you need skills of some sort first? What do you mean about him being caught by the sun?'

'Your skin.' Jay said, 'The sun did that cos you're not used to it yet. It'll sting for a bit.'

'You should be fine,' Seb commented, speaking at the same time as his brother. 'Depending on what it is you want to do. I mean, I had some experience of working in healing and I was happy to continue, but I wasn't forced. So I guess, unless you want to be a surgeon right off you should be ok. I've got some stuff that'll help your skin too.'

Chris was about to ask what a surgeon was, but was silenced by Jay announcing 'Food!' They all stood up and made their way to the serving tables.

After he'd eaten, Chris was feeling much more like himself again. He enjoyed listening to the tales of what Bertram and the others had been up to. He noticed too that none of them called him Bertram, always Bertie or

Bert. Bertram's face said he wasn't impressed. Chris didn't get many chances to join in the conversation, but he told himself that was alright, he'd had an interesting day and he might get chance to talk with Bertram alone sometime this evening. Then someone slapped him on the back and he almost choked on his batu. Turning he saw one of the men from the tannery grinning at him.

'Alright?' the man asked. 'Enjoy yourself today?'

'Yeah….it was really interesting, thanks.' Chris was stunned that the man remembered him.

'See ya around then,' the man waved and made his way to another table.

'Who was that?' Bertram asked.

'He works in the tannery,' Chris replied, quietly pleased that someone had recognised him and had come to say hello.

'You going to work in there then?' Bert asked with a sneer. 'The lads say it stinks!'

'It does,' Chris agreed. 'I don't think it's for me, but they were doing some beautiful work making harnesses and shoes and so on.'

Bertram shrugged and turned back to his work mates.

Chris looked at the back of Bertram's head, hurt and confused by his friend's attitude. Jay caught his eye and smiled, mouthing 'are you ok?' Chris nodded and tried to smile back.

***

Gradually the tables emptied and a huge firepit was

lit. Brewers heaved a couple of barrels onto a table, along with several jugs of wine and were soon surrounded by people wanting their wares.

Chris, Bertram and the others drifted along with the crowds. Bertram and Jay went to sit with their workmates, Chris could hear Jay arguing that they should have stopped with him. Bertram's reply was lost in the growing chatter of the crowd. Seb found his workmates and wandered away, leaving Chris standing alone and feeling rather lost. He had just decided to go back to their accommodation and get some sleep when he saw Anilla making her way towards him. As she reached him a heavy arm landed across his shoulders and he looked round into the face of one of the paper makers.

'Now then young man,' the man said. 'Ready for the fun, are you? Was good seeing your interest today, maybe we'll see more of you soon?' Chris saw uneven teeth smiling through the beard. He gave Chris a brief shake before wandering off in search of his mate.

Chris, shocked, turned to Anilla. 'What just happened?' he asked, shaking his head.

'I think they like you. They've already spoken to Fallaren about you,' she said, looking pleased.

'Oh!' Chris felt his mouth fall open. 'Is that good?'

'Let's hope so.' Anilla said.

Just then, somewhere in the darkness, a chord was struck on a guitar and silence rippled through the crowds.

'Come on, let's get seats,' Anilla whispered and the two of them slipped round the edges of the gathered folk before sliding in a gap and sitting on the floor. Anilla looked around expectantly and Chris was just about to ask what was going on when flares were lit. He saw they were bunches of the reeds he'd seen being gathered earlier, bound in big metal cups. The light they gave showed a raised stage and Fallaren standing in the middle of it, holding his hands up for attention.

Just like Tolson Chris thought, his heart sinking a little.

'Good evening.' Fallaren's voice carried over the crowd. 'For those of you who don't already know, we have a couple of lads with us now who've come from Salutem. Anyone originally from Salutem who wishes, please make yourselves known to Bert and Chris, I'm sure they'd appreciate any advice you can give them about settling in here. Welcome boys, we hope you'll be very happy here with us.'

The crowd cheered good naturedly and Chris, suddenly glad of the gloom, felt himself blushing. *OK, so not like Tolson* he thought with relief, smiling shyly at the folk who were looking with interest at him. A couple of rows in front he saw Bertram, his face set like stone as Fallaren shortened his name. Chris could see Jay attempting to calm him down.

On the stage Fallaren disappeared to be replaced by some of the crafters Chris had met earlier. They all had instruments, there were a couple of guitars, one man had a long whistle and there were tambourines and a couple of drums and, Chris gasped, two men had violins. He had only seen a violin once before and it was handled with reverence in Salutem. It was an antique relic; he had never heard it played. It was only kept as a reminder of how talented the craftsmen of old had been. Now, he was to hear not one, but two of them. They began playing and singing, and everyone joined in.

Although Chris didn't know any of the songs, he enjoyed the feeling which grew in the crowd. The songs rolled along, becoming livelier and livelier and before long people were up dancing.

'Does this sort of thing happen often?' Chris asked Anilla during one of the quiet moments between songs.

'Yeah, once or twice a week, especially in the good weather,' she said casually.

'Weather?'

'It's our name for if it's sunny and warm, or raining, or cold,' Anilla replied.

Chris was confused, but the music and singing began again and he was swept up in the camaraderie exuding from the crowd around him.

***

The moon was high in the sky before the evening drew to a close. The instruments were packed away, the beer barrels, now much lighter, were put onto the cart which had brought them, ready to be taken back by the brewers in the morning, and everyone drifted away to their quarters for the night. Several people shouted good night to Chris as he walked down the street with Anilla.

They reached his door and Anilla bid him good night. 'I'll come find you after breakfast,' she said. 'We've one more visit to make before you decide anything. Sleep well.'

Chris entered the hut to discover he was the first one back. He was ready for bed before Bertram and Jay came in. It looked like they'd been arguing.

'Hi,' Chris said, a little warily.

'Hi,' Jay said. 'What'd you make of your first proper evening here?'

'It was great!' Chris said with enthusiasm. 'I feel like I could sleep for a week, but I really enjoyed it.' His smile lit his face.

'Seems everyone knows who you are.' Bertram said sourly.

'Fallaren told 'em all.' Chris said, surprised.

'He's fed up, cos no one said anything to him, but he saw loads of folks talking to you.' Jay said with a look at Bertram that told him he disapproved of his attitude.

'Only 'cos I went round everywhere today,' Chris said reasonably. 'They remembered seeing me with Anilla, that's all. Everyone was really nice, very friendly. I like it.'

Bertram grumbled under his breath while he got ready for sleep. 'Is there anything can be done about my arms?' he demanded irritably. 'I thought you said Seb had some stuff to stop them hurting.'

'Yeah, Seb has salve,' Jay said shortly. 'He won't be long.' He turned away from Bertram and began getting ready for bed.

Seb arrived shortly afterwards and, taking one look at Bertram's face, handed him a pot of salve. 'Smear this on your arms and face where they're red,' he said. 'It should take the sting out and help them to feel less tight. When you're done, give it to Chris, looks like he could use it too.'

Bertram snatched the salve. 'Thanks,' he muttered before smearing himself generously with the translucent, greasy concoction. When he'd finished he put the pot on the table and climbed into bed.

Chris wandered over and helped himself to salve. The relief on his arms was almost immediate. 'Thanks Seb,' he said. 'That feels better already.'

'Leave it on the table,' Seb said. 'You can use it in the morning before you go out, it'll help protect you.'

Chris finished his face, peering in the mirror to make sure he covered the pink patches on his nose and chin. Then he put the cover over the pot and climbed exhausted into his bed. Sleep took a while to find him though, his mind was full of Taivas and her eggs, of the way he had been welcomed by most of the folk he'd encountered that day, and the unusual attention he'd received from the paper makers. With music still swirling in his head he slowly drifted off to sleep.

Chapter 5 - Decisions

The following morning after breakfast, Chris took all the dishes to the tent for cleaning and went back to the table he'd been sitting at to wait for Anilla. But it wasn't Anilla who found him. It was Narilka.

'Good morning Chris,' she said, sliding onto the bench next to him. 'How are you finding things here in Portum?'

Chris gave her a nervous smile. 'I really like it, thank you,' he said. 'Although,' he added more quietly. 'I'm still getting used to no walls and roof.' He looked sheepish. 'And the sun.' He said, rubbing the back of his neck.

Narilka laughed. 'You'll soon settle in,' she said. 'Can't beat the fresh air and some sun on your back. I hear your tour yesterday went well; did you enjoy it?'

'Yes,' Chris nodded. 'It was really interesting. All these different crafts, it's mind boggling.'

Narilka paused. 'That's a good thing, is it?'

'Yes,' Chris said, smiling.

'Fallaren and I have been approached by four different crafts, all offering you work with them. One actually demanding you join them,' she said. 'It seems you made a good impression. I...we...are very pleased.'

Chris was happy but he could feel heat rushing up his face. 'Where do you want me to work then?' he asked.

'That is for you to decide,' she said, standing up.

'Here comes Anilla, she will talk you through it all and help you. Although I understand you still have one more stop on your tour before any final decision is made.' She handed a piece of folded parchment to Anilla, then, with a nod, she left.

Anilla watched the leader walking away, a frown creasing her brow. 'You've made quite the impression,' she said, turning to Chris.

'Aren't they like this with everyone?' Chris asked.

'Nope,' Anilla shook her head. 'Never known it before.' She sank onto the bench opposite and looked closely at him. 'What have you told Bertram about our day yesterday?'

'Not much really,' Chris said sadly. 'He didn't seem very interested in what I'd been doing, he was more bothered about pipes and things. He wasn't very nice about it really, and last night he seemed jealous that folk were talking to me and not him.'

Anilla nodded. 'That's what I'd heard too,' she said quietly. 'He's being bossy with the others he's working with, and it's not going down too well. Although I hear he's come up with some good ideas so maybe his attitude will be worth it.'

'He was always in charge, back in Salutem,' Chris said. 'He was the supervisor, although I'm sure that was because his dad is one of the leaders.'

'Ah!' Anilla breathed. 'That would explain a lot. Want another cup of batu before we sort our day out?' When he nodded, she rose and went to the serving table, where large jugs were steaming. Fixing drinks for them both she wandered back to Chris and sat down, apparently deep in thought.

'Are you ok? Is everything alright?' Chris asked.

'What? Oh, yes,' she gave him a shadow of a smile. 'Fallaren knows I took you to see the eggs. I'm not sure I should have done that.'

'Oh no! I hope I didn't get you in trouble!' Chris looked horrified. 'It was me that wanted to see the eggs.'

'You'll be alright, but I might be in hot water.' Anilla looked worried for the first time since he'd met her.

'We didn't do any harm, did we?' he asked her quietly.

'I don't think so,' she shook her head. 'Taivas didn't mind us being there.'

'She likes the lad,' said a deep voice.

Anilla jumped like she'd been scalded, and Chris turned to see Fallaren.

'I hope it wasn't wrong to take him, Fallaren,' Anilla said, hanging her head.

'I'd prefer it if we were given notice of any future visits,' he said. 'Sometimes the dragons get jumpy, but, as Taivas knows you, all is well. Saff says she likes you.' He looked at Chris. 'What did you make of your first encounter with a dragon, lad?'

'I was scared, she's so huge,' Chris stammered.

'He tried hiding behind me,' Anilla laughed, her confidence recovered.

'You're sorting out his work detail this morning?' he asked Anilla.

'Yes,' she said. 'Narilka told me several of the crafts want him, so it might take a while. And we've yet to visit the Tellers.'

'Good luck with that! I see you are well supplied,' Fallaren indicated their fresh drinks. He nodded at them and wandered away, shouting to a couple of men.

'Once we've finished our drinks, I'll take you over to meet the Tellers, then we can have a chat about what you'd like to do.' Anilla said, sipping her batu.

'What are tellers?' Chris wanted to know.

'Storytellers.' Anilla said. 'Remember I told you books and paper aren't in common use, even with our own crafters? Well, we still need to teach our young, and some of the not so young. So we have Tellers, who keep our history alive and teach reading and writing too. They usually play instruments, because a lot of folk prefer listening to teaching songs rather than a lecture.'

'We can probably miss them out then,' Chris said. 'I can't sing or play.' He took a swig of his batu. 'I really like this stuff you know,' he said. 'There's nothing like it back in Salutem.'

'Isn't there?' Anilla asked absently. 'Look, I think we ought to go to the Tellers, just for the look of things, you know, for Fallaren and Narilka if nothing else. Don't want them complaining that I've not done things right.'

Chris sighed. 'Alright.'

Anilla led the way deeper into the settlement proper, along streets and narrow pathways, until they came to a long, low building with several wide doors in the long side which faced the street.

'This is the school,' Anilla said. 'This is where the Tellers hold classes for our children during the day. They often entertain in the evenings too.' She pushed open the nearest door and Chris followed her inside.

They walked into a large, square room which held several rows of tables and chairs, most of which were filled with youngsters. At the front of the room a male Teller was singing in a strangely monotone voice. Chris listened to the tale of dragons chasing humans and breathing fire at them. As Anilla and Chris stood there the Teller paused.

'Here is one of our new arrivals,' he said in a surprisingly squeaky voice. 'Perhaps you would be good enough to talk to us about the caves you come from? What were you told about why humans were living in such a way?'

Chris, startled, began to back away but Anilla put a hand to his back and, gently but firmly, propelled him towards the Teller.

'We were told that there had been a war,' he said. 'Which meant the outside wasn't safe for people. We weren't told anything about dragons though, they said it was something called a nuclear war, with armies throwing bombs at each other, or something.' He was beginning to wish he'd paid closer attention to his own classes.

A small hand was in the air. 'Yes Shari?' the Teller said. 'You have a question?'

'Yeth,' the small girl lisped. 'You din't know nuffin' about dragons then?'

'No, I'm afraid not,' Chris smiled at her. 'They told us things to scare us, I suppose they were trying to keep us safe.' He gave a shrug.

'So you never questioned it?' the Teller asked.

'Of course he did Tark, that's why he's here!' Anilla sounded exasperated. Tark flushed. 'Anyway, we're here for Chris to have a look around and see what you guys do, ok? He's still trying to decide on an occupation.'

Tark nodded. 'Of course,' he mumbled. 'So nice to meet you Chris.'

'Likewise,' Chris nodded at him and glanced at the children, who were looking at him in wonder.

'Come on,' Anilla said quietly. 'Through this way are the workshops.' She led the way to a door at the rear of the classroom. As the door closed behind them Chris heard Tark begin singing again.

'He sounds really strange when he sings.'

'That's how the teaching songs are,' Anilla explained. 'No tune as such, more a rhythm, they usually have a drum to keep time.'

Chris looked around the room he found himself in. It was quiet in here, several benches held instruments in various states of manufacture. Chris recognised a violin.

'Wow,' he said, going over to the bench and stroking the fine wood reverently. 'We had one in Salutem you know, but it was ancient, a relic. They kept it wrapped up in soft cloths and only brought it out to show us on special days. I never heard one played until last night, it was fantastic!'

'Glad you enjoyed it,' said a voice from the corner of the room and a Teller stood up from behind a bench. 'Max, pleased to meet you.' The tall, muscular man stepped around the bench and came to Chris, holding out his hand. 'I am also from Salutem,' he said, gripping Chris' forearm firmly.

Chris gripped Max's arm in return. 'You...you're from Salutem? I don't remember you at all, when did you get out?'

'I escaped fifteen years ago. Fallaren found me near the river, took pity on me and brought me here.'

'Fallaren did?' Chris was impressed.

'He wasn't the leader back then,' Anilla chipped in. 'He used to go on expeditions looking for herbs and plants. That's how we found Chris and Bert,' she told Max.

'It's nice to meet someone who understands what it was like in Salutem,' Chris said. 'Although it's already starting to feel like a bad dream, and I only left two days ago!' He shook his head.

'I know what you mean,' Max said. 'You think you might want to be a Teller then?'

'I don't know,' Chris said slowly, 'I have no musical talent and I doubt I could make beautiful instruments like these.'

'We're going to go through his interests when we get back to the tables,' Anilla said. 'See what he wants to do and where he thinks he'd be best placed.'

'I'm always on the lookout for new Tellers,' Max said. 'Full training is given.' His eyes twinkled at Chris.

'As it is in every profession,' Anilla said crossly. 'He'll do very well, wherever he chooses to work.'

Chris wished he shared her optimism.

From the next room came an almighty crash and Max rushed through the door, which led to another workshop. A young man was standing in the middle of the room, hundreds of fragments of flat, black stone surrounding him.

'What have I told you?' Max shouted. 'You sure you don't want to work with us?' he said to Chris. 'We could use the help.'

The young man, blushing furiously, hung his head. 'Sorry Max,' he mumbled. 'It just slipped out of my hands.'

'The miners are going to go mad,' Max said, before relenting. 'But to be fair, it's not a long leap for most of them. Get this swept up. I'll order more slate.'

The boy went to find a brush as Anilla began ushering Chris from the building. 'We'd best be off now,' she said to Max. 'Fallaren wants to know Chris' decision today. See you later.' She shut the door behind them and began walking back the way they'd come.

'I had to show you the Tellers,' she said. 'But I wouldn't recommend it for you. Although it might be nice to have someone from Salutem to talk to.' She looked at Chris. 'What do you think?'

'I think I'd rather not be the one responsible for dropping a load of whatever that was, and risking Max and the miners yelling at me,' he said.

They made their way back to the dining area and Chris got them both drinks while Anilla settled at a table and pulled out the list of crafts which had expressed interest in having Chris work with them. He sat opposite her and grinned.

'OK, let's have it,' he said. 'Who wants me?'

'Firstly, what are your thoughts? Did any of the crafts interest you sufficiently for you to give them a try?'

'There were a couple,' Chris said thoughtfully. 'I liked the brewers; I think that would be interesting work. And I really liked the idea of making paper and books, even if they were grumpy.' He gave Anilla a grin. 'I didn't have any special training in Salutem really, nothing that I want to carry on at least, so I'm open to trying new things.'

Anilla's face gave nothing away. 'Shall we go through the list?'

Top was the tannery.

'What?! They can't really have liked me, I was holding my breath most of the time,' Chris said, horrified.

Anilla chuckled. 'I think they try for everyone,' she said, putting a line through the tannery offer. 'They struggle to find apprentices, but it's a necessary profession.'

Next were the brewers, which Chris was quite pleased about. 'I liked it in there,' he said. 'I reckon I could work with them.'

'I'll leave them on the list for now, shall I?'

Chris nodded. 'Who's next?'

'The fishers,' Anilla told him. 'Seems they liked your attitude and your energy.' She looked at the grimace on his face. 'I take it that's another 'no' then?'

'No! Definitely no!' Chris wrinkled his nose. 'Why do all the smelly professions want me?'

'You showed interest and you were polite,' Anilla said. 'I'm sure they don't expect you to work with them, but at least you know they noticed you taking an interest.'

Chris nodded. 'OK, who's the last?' He braced himself, quietly sure that he would be going to work for the brewers before the day was out.

'Are you ready for this?' Anilla asked. 'The paper crafters.'

'What?' Chris stared at her. His mind whirled with the possibilities. Working with them would be special he thought. Paper and books were unusual, high worth items, that worth might rub off onto the folk who made them. He sat; head tilted to one side as he thought. He didn't place the same importance on rank as Bertram did, but still, making paper, learning how to create books. That would be interesting.

Chris' eyes were sparkling now. He sat, drinking his batu, thinking of how his life might be if he joined that select band at the other side of the river. 'When do I have to decide?'

'Today, preferably, but if you really can't make up your mind, I'm sure we could arrange for you to do a day or two in each place, like a trial, so you can see what you would be expected to do.' Anilla was watching him closely, pretty sure she knew what he was going to say. She hid a smile behind her mug and watched him over the rim.

'I think,' Chris said slowly. 'That I'd like to give paper making a try.'

Anilla nodded. 'Good choice,' she said. 'I'll just...'

But what she was about to say was drowned out by the sound of a loud bell being rung repeatedly. The sound came from the pass in the hills beyond the dragon caves. Chris barely had time to register the noise before Portum was full of people, clearly scared, running for cover. Anilla grabbed him by the arm and forced him to run with her to the nearest building.

'What's happening?' he panted.

'Dragons,' came the terse reply.

Everyone in the place was silent. It seemed their collective breath was being held. Above them Chris could hear roars and shouting. A sharp scream pierced the air, making him wince.

'Wild dragons are attacking,' Anilla told him in a whisper. 'Our dragons and their riders are defending Portum.'

Chris looked at her, eyes wide. 'Does this happen often?' he asked, wondering if this were the reason Tolson and the other elders had insisted the outside world was unsafe for people.

Anilla shrugged, trying to appear casual in spite of the obvious tension among the folk of Portum. 'A few times a month I suppose,' she said. 'But our dragons always see them off, don't worry.'

'We just have to keep quiet,' hissed a voice.

They stood in silence for what felt like a long time, then another bell rang. This time there was a series of three rings followed by a pause.

'All clear,' Anilla translated for him.

Chris left the building and looked to the skies.

Dragons were overhead, their riders calling to one another. Some were heading back to the caves, others were flying in patterns, making sure the wild dragons were all gone. The huge beasts were surprisingly agile, turning on a wing tip. Chris watched, mesmerised.

'Don't go getting any ideas,' said a familiar voice behind him. He turned to see Bertram. 'You won't get to be a rider,' he said. 'Stop wasting your time with day dreams.'

'I...I wasn't thinking about that at all,' Chris stuttered, face flushing angrily. 'I was only admiring them.'

Bertram's look said he didn't believe him. 'I'm off back to my work now,' he said. 'As you don't have any work I suppose you're staying here, are you?'

'No, Bert, he's not,' Anilla said firmly. 'He starts his own work today, he's been offered work by several crafts, he's just deciding which one, aren't you Chris?'

Chris was thankful for her intervention. 'Yeah, we were just going through it when the alarm sounded.'

Bertram looked sceptical but left them to it, calling to Jay and a couple of others to wait for him, before jogging to catch them up as they didn't seem to hear him.

'And he was your best friend in Salutem?' Anilla asked softly.

'He wasn't like this back there,' Chris said, ready to defend, then he paused. 'Actually, he always was, a bit, I suppose. But he knew his job, and I was just learning, so I never questioned his superiority. Anilla, why does no one here use his full name?'

'Don't they? I suppose Bertram is quite a mouthful and we tend to shorten things. I usually answer to Annie.'

Anilla said. 'Let's hope you find nicer friends here.'

'I already have!' Chris said. 'You're my friend, aren't you?'

Anilla looked pleased and nodded. 'Yes, I'm your friend Chris,' she said. 'Now, want more batu while we finalise your work decision?'

'That'd be good, bet ours went cold while we were in there,' Chris said, 'and maybe you can tell me more about dragons?' He tried not to sound over eager, but it was hard to keep the excitement from his voice.

Anilla grabbed them both drinks and settled herself opposite him. She handed him a steaming mug. 'If anyone asks, we're talking crafts, ok?'

Chris grinned and nodded.

'Good, now, I guess you want to know about the wilds?'

'Yeah, I mean, how many are there?'

'There are hundreds near here. They were hunted once, for their hides and meat and, I suppose because they were attacking domestic herds.' Anilla said. 'We still have some books in our archives which have dragonhide covers,' she added.

'I suppose, if you killed a dragon, back then, you would be a hero, or something,' Chris said. 'Especially as there were no tame dragons, must have been incredibly dangerous.'

'You're probably right,' Anilla said. 'You've seen how our riders are treated, but we have them to thank for keeping us safe.'

'Do you think I have what it takes to become a rider, one day?' He asked.

'I don't know,' Anilla replied. 'A lot of things are monitored before you're put up for a chance of being a rider. How hard you work, how well you settle in here. Your character needs to show itself really. Don't be in a hurry though, having a dragon to look after is hard work!'

'Do riders have to stop their usual work?' Chris asked.

'For a while they do,' she told him. 'When Saff was paired with Taivas she was excused all other duties for a full six months, until Taivas was old enough to be on her own for a while. They're like babies at first you know, they even sleep with their riders. They curl up like big dogs next to their people. Saff loves it.'

'So after the six months, do riders go back to their normal jobs?'

'Yes, as much as they can, but of course dragon care must be the priority. Most only work part of the day so they can train and do...whatever it is that's needed. There's a lot of bathing and feeding as I understand it,' she laughed.

Chris grinned, 'I'm looking forward to seeing a hatching,' he said. 'It must be exciting.'

'Oh it is!' Anilla said, her smile lighting her eyes. 'Everyone goes you know, and when a member of your family gets chosen it's so special. Everyone knows riders are brave and they have to be so dedicated. It's such an honour.' Anilla's eyes were bright with pride.

'Do you want to be a rider?' he asked.

Anilla lowered her eyes. 'I'd love nothing more,' she said.

Chris was quiet for a moment, sipping his batu and thinking. 'Is there a best age, for becoming a rider?' he asked falteringly. He realised he had no idea how old Anilla was.

'I don't think so,' she said with a shrug. 'I've been to hatchings where young boys have been chosen at the same time as men in their late twenties. There's no sense in the choosing you know, the dragons like someone, and that's pretty much it. Over the years the leaders have tried to anticipate what the baby dragons will want in a person but dragons are a law to themselves. Now, it's based on understanding and hard work.'

Chris nodded, this made sense. He finished his drink. 'Now, how do I go about becoming a maker of paper?' He asked.

'Well, we'll go and find Fallaren or Narilka, and they will give you your coin,' she said.

Chris looked blankly at her.

'You're given a coin, a metal disc, to give to your crafting master,' she explained. 'The coin is yours, and if you don't like your chosen craft you must ask the master for your coin back in order to be released and find another job.'

'Ok,' Chris still looked confused. Portum ways made no sense to him. 'Let's go then.' He stood up and collected their mugs.

***

They found Narilka in the big building which

Anilla told him was the Council Hall, she was talking to a group of men about some cloth they had brought her. When she spotted Chris and Anilla she excused herself and came towards them.

'Hello Chris,' she said. 'Have you made your decision?'

'Yes, I think so,' he said, hoping his choice would meet with approval.

'Chris has decided he'd like to join the paper crafters,' Anilla said.

'An excellent choice,' Narilka said. 'Could you take him into the office please Anilla, and I will join you shortly.'

Anilla nodded and, taking Chris by the arm, encouraged him to walk with her towards a doorway at the side of the building. This led into a smaller room which contained a huge desk, and a couple of large, padded chairs. The desk was piled with scrolls and a couple of thick, heavy books. On one side of the room was a set of shelves which held books, some of them so old the covers were cracking. Chris had never seen so many in one place before.

'Wow!' he breathed, bending closer to inspect the titles.

'Don't touch them,' Anilla whispered urgently.

'I wouldn't,' Chris said. 'I was brought up to think of books as ancient relics, far too important for the likes of me to handle.'

The door opened and Narilka appeared. It was the first time Chris had seen her annoyed. He straightened up immediately and stepped away from the bookshelves.

'Sometimes I wonder if I'm wasting my breath!' Narilka threw herself into one of the chairs and let out a huge sigh before pulling a scroll towards her and locating her pen. Looking up she caught the expression on Chris' face and glanced questioningly at Anilla. 'Is everything alright?' she asked.

'He thought he might be in trouble for looking so closely at your books,' Anilla explained.

'Oh! I hadn't even noticed,' Narilka said. 'Feel free to look, especially as it's your profession of choice. Who knows, you may even be able to renew the bindings on some of them in due course.'

Chris, lost for words, could feel the blush starting to creep up his neck and lowered his head, hoping she wouldn't notice.

Narilka saw him flushing and, hiding a smile, began writing on her scroll, giving him time to recover himself.

'Anilla, if I give you his letter and coin, would you like to go with him and speak to Garad and Edwin?'

'Yes, of course,' Anilla nodded.

'Good, thank you,' Narilka said, still writing. 'I know they can be, er, difficult sometimes, but they have asked for the boy to join them. Hopefully they won't give you any trouble. There!' She signed the document with a flourish and blotted it before folding it neatly, sealing it with melted wax and stamping it with her seal. Chris, who had been trying to read the letter upside down, was disappointed.

Next she unlocked a drawer in the desk and took out a small bag which clinked as she laid it on the desk. Loosening the cord at the neck, she extracted a metal coin, it was a dull silver in colour and had a design marked on it. 'This is yours Chris,' she said, showing him the coin on the palm of her hand. 'You give it to your craft master when you begin working with them. If you ever feel you need to leave their craft, you must ask for it to be returned to you, for you cannot begin in a new craft without it. Understand?' She handed both items to Anilla.

'Yes, thank you. I won't let you down,' he said, his voice wobbling slightly.

Narilka sat back and looked at him. 'This is all still very new, isn't it? And I suppose this makes it seem very final. I know you miss your family and friends, but I hope that Portum and the people here will make it easier for you to forge your new life with us.'

Chris nodded. 'Everyone's been very nice and kind,' he said, desperately trying not to burst into tears. 'But you're right, I do miss my old home and my family.'

'Of course you do! It's only natural. I remember when I first got here,' Narilka said. 'It took me a few months before I truly felt at home, and now look at me.' She smiled broadly. 'Of one thing I am sure, young Chris, you will do very well here. You have the right attitude and we, that is Fallaren and I, are very happy to have you with us. Now, off you go you two, I have men to supervise.'

Anilla and Chris left the room. In the main hall a group of nervous looking men jumped when they opened the door before resuming their hushed conversation, continually glancing in the direction of Narilka's office.

Narilka watched them leave with a thoughtful expression, then she reached over for the ledger she used to keep track of work details and began to make notes.

Outside, Chris relaxed a little. 'I thought I was going to cry when she mentioned my family,' he said to Anilla. 'I hadn't realised Narilka wasn't born here!'

'No, she arrived when she was about fifteen or sixteen, I think,' Anilla told him. 'But, like you, she got here with the attitude that she was going to fit in and make a new life for herself. And she was very successful at it too!'

'Can I see that coin she gave you?' Chris asked.

'Sure. Not sure why she gave it to me anyway,' Anilla handed him the coin. 'Usually you must make your own way to your work.'

'Perhaps it's because they aren't usually very friendly?' He hazarded.

'I guess, but they asked for you, insisted really, so I don't think you'll get any trouble. Never mind, I'm glad to walk with you, your last act as a newcomer. After this you'll be Chris the papermaker.'

He felt his stomach jump at her words as he inspected the coin. The dull metal disc had a hole in the centre and a design around it showing dragons. He handed it back. 'You'd best keep it for now,' he said. 'Narilka might ask them who had it when we get there.'

'Why would she?'

Chris shrugged. 'I'm used to being watched all the time,' he said. 'You get used to having to think like that.'

Anilla took the coin from him, shaking her head

sadly. 'I'm sorry it was so bad for you back there,' she said.

'I guess I made it worse for myself by challenging them. They had me thrown in prison, then I was followed...watched. Some woman trailed after me and listened into every conversation I had.' He sighed. 'It was difficult.'

'No wonder you wanted to get away,' Anilla said.

'Yeah,' Chris nodded, 'I'm glad I escaped. Although I miss my family, I do like it here. I'm glad I'm in Portum.'

They made their way across the river to the paper making building. On arriving, they heard deep voices withing, a rumbling conversation.

Anilla raised her hand to rap on the door, pausing to mouth at Chris, 'Ready?'

When he nodded mutely, she gave the door a smart rap before opening it and walking in. Chris followed her inside, blinking in the gloom as his eyes adjusted.

'I've brought you a new apprentice,' Anilla said brightly. 'Garad, here's his coin and letter from Narilka,' she handed them over to the older man, who was glowering at the intrusion.

'Oh. It's you, is it?' Garad looked from Anilla to Chris.

Turning to Chris, Anilla said, 'I hope you'll be happy here, don't let this miserable pair turn you sour!' Then she retreated and the door closed behind her.

Chris turned to his new work colleagues, unsure of how they would take to this interruption of their routine, to find both men watching him.

'Pleased to have you with us lad,' Garad said, holding out his hand to Chris.

Chris shook the hand, 'I'm really happy you wanted me to work with you,' he said, 'I find it fascinating.'

'You won't!' Edwin said with a sharp laugh, 'give it a couple of days.' He and Garad laughed heartily and Chris looked in bewilderment from one to the other.

'You're from Salutem then?' Garad said, giving Chris a strange look. 'Edwin and meself hail from there too. Been here a long time now.'

'You're both from Salutem? I used to think no one else had made it out before Bertram and me. They certainly kept it quiet! I've met three or four folk now.' Chris shook his head in wonder.

'Ay well, I daresay they wouldn't advertise it, would they?' Edwin said. 'Be like inviting a mass exodus, and then who would they have to boss around?'

'Right lad let's get you started off. No time for chit chat.' Garad threw the coin and letter on his table with scant regard for their value and led Chris to the back corner of the room, where several lengths of tree were stacked. 'First job, these need the bark stripping. You use one of these,' he hefted a lethal looking instrument and gave Chris a quick demonstration of its use. 'Now you have a go.'

Several minutes later Chris had sweat running down his face and the section of tree looked as though it had been chewed. 'You made it look so easy!' he gasped.

Garad laughed, 'I've had years of practice lad, you'll get it though. Keep going, they all need doing.' He wandered back to his own work, leaving Chris to struggle with his task.

At the end of a very long day Garad wandered over and examined Chris' handiwork. Splinters of tree covered the floor, the bench and his new apprentice. 'You're getting there laddie,' he said gruffly, 'you've made less mess than Edwin did on his first day. Come over here a minute.'

Chris followed Garad to his table, where the coin and letter still lay. Garad scooped them up and pulled a key from his pocket. He unlocked a drawer in the table and put them in it before removing a small object which he handed unceremoniously to Chris. 'Your pin,' he said, 'if you still want to be apprenticed here that is.'

Chris looked at the pin. It was a large version of the safety pins he'd seen used by some healers in Salutem to hold bandages. This pin was ornamental though, it held a bar of some shiny metal and set into the metal was a white stone. 'Is that a quartz?' he breathed.

'That it is lad.' Garad nodded. 'Sign of an apprentice that is, and see the shape of the setting?'

'A scroll. Is that the symbol of the paper craft?'

'It is indeed, well done.' Garad was wearing a broad grin.

Carefully, Chris put the badge in his pocket. 'No point putting it on this,' he flapped his filthy shirt, 'I'll wait until I get home and pin it to my jacket, like you two do.'

Chapter 6 – Making Paper

The sun was setting as Garad, Edwin and Chris left the paper crafters hut. There was an easy-going camaraderie between them which, given their reputation, surprised Chris. His head was spinning with new knowledge; with words like deckle and furnish, couching and pulping. He had spent the day learning how to break down tree fibres in the first stage of paper making. His arms and back were aching but he had never been happier.

He bid so-long to his new colleagues and went to his accommodation to wash and change ready for the evening meal. His shirt was covered in fragments of tree pulp, which stuck to everything. Remembering his new apprentice pin, he took it from his pocket and put it on his bed. He had just put a clean shirt on when Bertram and Jay came through the doorway.

'Hey stranger!' Jay cried. 'Where were you at lunch-time? We missed you.'

'Oh, I had lunch at work.' Chris told him. 'It's a bit of a walk to come all the way in, so we need to take ours with us. They shared with me today.'

'Where have they put you?' Bertram asked, struggling out of his clothes and dumping them in a pile on the floor.

'I told you, they don't 'put' you anywhere, you get to choose,' Jay told him, rolling his eyes at Chris.

'I'm working with the paper makers,' Chris told them.

Bertram's head whipped round. 'You're what? How did you land that gig? I thought they were really picky!'

'They are.' Chris said. 'They wanted me, asked Fallaren for me. But I still had the choice.' He didn't mention the other offers he'd received. Best not to irritate Bertram any more.

'That's fantastic!' Jay was happy enough for all of them. 'You learned any trade secrets yet?'

'Yup, but they're secret, can't tell the likes of you.' Chris grinned at him.

'Fair enough, fair enough. You off to dinner? You do still eat with us commoners, don't you?'

'I'll consider it,' Chris was enjoying this, it was almost as good as being with the gang back in Salutem.

'Wait for us then,' Jay said. 'Won't be a minute, if Bertie gets a move on that is.'

Bertram, grumbling, moved over to allow Jay access to the washing station, and before long they were all sauntering in the direction of the big square and a good, hot meal.

***

Once they had taken their seats, the interrogation began in earnest.

'What's it like working with them? Everyone says they're the most miserable pair in Portum?' Jay said. 'Do you think you'll like it? What's the work like? Is it difficult? Are they alright really? How hard is it to make a book?'

Chris could hardly get a word in. 'They're not

miserable!' he said when Jay paused for breath. 'They just don't like being interrupted. It's delicate work.' He thought for a moment, recalling the brute force required to strip the bark. 'You need to focus; it could be dangerous if you lose concentration at the wrong time. If my hand had slipped when I was removing the bark I could have lost a finger...or an arm.'

Bertram looked up. 'Are you sure you should be doing work like that? It doesn't sound safe at all,' he said.

'It's fine, as long as you're careful and keep your focus on what you're doing.' Chris countered.

Jay had news of his own. 'We're almost done with the first stage of the pipework,' he said. 'Won't be long till we're all sent off to different areas for work.'

Bertram looked at Jay sharply. 'What do you mean?' he asked. 'I thought this job would take months.'

'Oh, it probably will,' Jay said. 'But we won't be doing it. The Smiths will carry on. They take care of all the technical stuff, we're just the hired muscle.'

'Smiths?' Bertram queried.

'They're the crafters who deal with metal work and gems and so on,' Chris said. 'I saw their place over by the mines, but Anilla didn't take me right the way across to them. I think they make jewellery too, she said something about rings and cloak pins.'

Jay nodded, waving a chunk of bread at him. 'That's right! They're the ones with the metal know how. They've got lads who know about electrics and motors and whatnot.'

'What will you do when this job of yours is done

then?' Chris asked.

'I suppose I'll go back to the fishery, that's what I was doing before, but I didn't like it much.' Jay sighed. 'That's why I volunteered for this job.'

'Can't you ask for your coin and go do something else then?' Chris asked.

'Yeah, I could, but I don't know what.' Jay said.

Bertram looked confused. 'What are you talking about?' he demanded. 'What's this about coins?'

'When you start a job here, you're given a coin. It's a metal disc you give to the master of the craft. If you don't like what you're doing, you can ask for it back and go work somewhere else.' Chris looked at Jay for confirmation.

Jay nodded. 'I was training to weave back home,' he said. 'But I said I wanted to try something different when I got here, just not sure fishing is it,' he laughed. 'I'll have a think about it. Might have to surrender my pin and ask for my coin back.'

'What job will I be given?' Bertram sounded concerned. 'I mean, pipes and pumps is what I was doing before, and I don't really want to change.'

'Then see if you can work with the Smiths,' Chris suggested. 'Stands to reason really, if they're the ones who do that sort of stuff.'

Bertram nodded thoughtfully, chewing slowly. He was quiet until they had finished eating.

Chris had just cleared his plate when a hand landed on his shoulder and a grey beard appeared by his cheek. 'Evenin' laddie,' said a gravelly voice. 'Enjoy your first day did ya?'

Chris turned to see Garad, with Edwin standing behind him. 'Yeah, it wasn't too bad,' Chris said, 'I reckon I could put up with it for a bit.'

Garad and Edwin roared with laughter and Garad slapped him on the back. 'Ah, ye'll do for me, you will. See you in the morning lad.'

Chris turned back to the table to see a look of shock on Jay's face.

'Never seen either of them smile before,' he said. 'Much less laugh, what have you done to 'em?'

Chris shrugged, 'I was just interested in the work,' he said. 'They're alright really.'

'Wonder if they'd consider another apprentice,' Jay said dreamily.

'That'd be great,' Chris said. 'Want me to have a word?'

'Yeah,' Jay nodded. 'I think I'd like that,' he thought for a moment. 'Not smelly in there is it?'

'No.' Chris laughed. 'But it's harder work than you might think.'

Bertram sat up. 'I might ask about it too,' he said. 'It seems to be a highly esteemed craft, elite you could say.' Jay pulled a face at Chris. Bertram didn't notice. 'I think, as it's only a small craft too, it would be easier to rise through the ranks. I think my dad would approve, don't you Chris?'

'What? Oh, yeah, maybe,' Chris said. 'I'm not so sure he'd like you doing all the graft, you know, stripping tree trunks down and beating them to pulp.'

'How many Smith crafters are there?' Bertram asked Jay in an apparent change of heart.

'Dunno,' Jay replied helpfully. 'You could try asking Anilla, she seems to know everything. I'm sure Narilka and Fallaren are training her up to be leader one day.'

This made Bertram sit up. 'The leaders aren't voted for by the people then? It's not hereditary either?'

'Nah, as far as I can tell they get to choose folk and train them.' Jay shrugged. 'I could be wrong though, not been here long meself,' he reminded Bertram.

Bertram stood up and looked around, before darting away suddenly.

'He's a right one, your mate,' Jay said. 'Very concerned about rank, isn't he?'

'He was always the same,' Chris said. 'Never quite as bad as this though.'

They could hear Bertram's strident voice now and looked around to see him talking to Anilla. She was shaking her head, speaking quietly as usual, and Bertram was getting louder. People around them were turning to see what was going on, and a man stood up to interrupt. Chris could just make out that he was telling Bertram now wasn't the time or place for these discussions.

Anilla took the opportunity to duck away and she headed straight for Chris.

'Are you ok?' he asked, noticing she was shaking.

'Yes,' Anilla sat next to him. 'He's not very friendly, is he?' Her breath caught as she spoke.

'He's changed since we got out,' Chris said. 'He was never like this back in Salutem.'

'He had daddy's backing there though, didn't he?' Anilla said quietly. 'No one questioned him I bet.'

'No,' Chris said. 'Not really, he was who he was, but he was always up for a laugh, and rebellious, always ready to get one over the higher ups. Now it seems he wants to be one of them.'

'Easy to rebel against your parents,' Jay said.

Bertram came storming back to the table and took in the scene. Anilla sitting close to Chris, Jay leaning in, talking quietly to them both. 'Oh, I see how it is!' He turned away and marched quickly in the direction of their living quarters.

'I wish they'd get him solo accommodation, fast!' Jay said with feeling. 'He's going to be impossible now.'

'I'll have a word,' Anilla said. 'It may be possible, although he'll be transferring to a craft soon, might not be a problem for long. What set all that off anyway?'

The boys told her how the conversation had gone and she sat, shaking her head in disbelief. 'He only wants to do what you're doing to prove he's better at it than you are, you know that don't you?' she said to Chris.

'That and it's what he calls high ranking, I think he feels he should be in charge of me. He always was in Salutem.' Chris said. 'I hope they don't let him in; I like it over there, it's interesting.'

'I'm not sure they want anyone else,' Anilla said. 'Sorry Jay,' she smiled at his disappointed face. 'But you can always ask, I'm sure Chris would put in a word for you, wouldn't you?'

Chris nodded. He'd rather work with Jay than Bertram.

The boys stood up reluctantly. 'Sorry, we have work in the morning,' Jay said to Anilla.

'And I've got to walk right the way over the other side of the river,' Chris said, trying to sound dismayed and failing.

'Off you go, you're quite right,' Anilla said to them. 'I hope he's not too moody with you tonight. Jay, come find me in the morning after breakfast, I'll see what I can sort out work wise for you if you don't want to go back to the fishery.'

Jay nodded and he and Chris began wending their way towards their beds.

'Do you really think she's being trained up for leader?' Chris asked.

'No idea, but she does seem to know everything, and everyone.' Jay said. 'She's nice though, I like her.'

They entered the hut quietly. Bertram was already in bed. He wasn't asleep, Chris could tell by his breathing, but he didn't move when they walked in and made no attempt to talk to them.

Chris found his pin where he'd left it on his bed. He picked it up and turned it slightly so it shone in the little light there was. He slipped it beneath his pillow and he and Jay readied themselves for bed as silently as possible and went to sleep.

Chapter 7 – A new smith

At breakfast the following morning, Chris, Bertram and Jay sat together, eating in silence as the previous evening hung over them. Bertram finished first and, without waiting for Jay, left the table and headed off to his work.

'Phew!' Jay let out a long breath. 'That was awkward!'

'It was,' Chris said sadly. 'I'm really surprised at him, although I shouldn't be. Salutem is all about rank, he hasn't figured out how Portum works yet.'

Anilla appeared at their table and slid onto the bench next to Chris.

'Good morning boys,' she said cheerfully. 'Guess what?'

'What?' they chorused.

'I've just been speaking to Fallaren,'

Jay and Chris exchanged glances. 'And?'

'He is now having a chat with Garad about maybe having Jay work with them.'

'Yes!' Jay looked triumphant.

'Nothing has been agreed yet,' she cautioned him. 'But you never know. In other news, the fishers are keen to have you back with them, they say you're a good worker and a quick learner. Fortunately, they made these comments where Fallaren and Garad could hear them...' she laughed.

'Brilliant.' Chris said. 'Fingers crossed eh?' He

caught two confused expressions and Jay began trying to cross his fingers.

'What does this do?' he asked, using his left hand to hold the fingers of his right hand in the crossed position.

'Nothing really,' Chris said. 'It's something we say to hope for good luck, or a good outcome.'

'Oh, superstition.' Jay said dismissively.

'Fallaren's coming over,' Anilla hissed.

Chris began stacking dirty dishes and Jay drained his mug.

'Boys,' Fallaren said, taking the empty place next to Jay. 'I've been hearing good things about the two of you.'

Chris glanced over towards Garad, who was deep in conversation with Edwin.

'Jay,' Fallaren continued. 'The fishers would very much like you to continue your work with them. However, Anilla has spoken with me about the events of last night. She tells me you're interested in joining the paper makers with young Chris?'

'Yes sir,' Jay nodded, glancing nervously at Chris.

'I've just spoken with Garad, and he is willing to give you a try. As this is just a trial there's no need to get your coin just yet, give it a day or two, then you can decide with Garad if it's right for you. Alright?'

'Thank you!' Jay almost shouted. 'That's brilliant,' he continued, regaining control of himself. 'I won't let you down Fallaren, Anilla, thank you.'

Fallaren got up to leave, 'I know you won't, you've

done well so far in Portum.' And he was gone, striding away towards the Council rooms.

Jay let out a whoop. 'Does this mean I'm not going back to work with Bashta and Bertie today then?' he asked Anilla.

'No,' she said. 'You're going off with Chris to make paper. I think Garad and Edwin are waiting for you,' she nudged Chris with her elbow.

'I see,' he said, standing and picking up their dirty dishes. 'C'mon then Jay, let's go to work.'

Anilla watched the pair trot towards the paper craftsmen, saw introductions being made, then the four left together. Scoria chased after them a moment later, handing them each a leather bag which Anilla knew held their lunches. With a satisfied smile, she turned and made her way to her bees.

***

The sky was darkening and vibrant shades of red and orange lit the distant hills when Jay and Chris returned to the village. Laughing and talking, they made their way straight to the eating area, handed in their lunch bags and grabbed plates.

'I'm famished,' Jay announced. 'Who'd have thought making paper would be such hungry work?'

'Mmhmm,' Chris agreed, his mouth already full, even though he hadn't finished filling his plate. 'When will I stop being so hungry?' he asked, swallowing his meat.

Jay grinned and shrugged, stuffing a whole, roasted potato into his mouth.

Together they made their way to a table and sat opposite each other. They were halfway through their meal when Bertram plonked himself down next to Chris.

'Where did you get to today?' he demanded of Jay. 'Bashta and me had to work extra cos you never showed up.'

'Fallaren gave me other work to do,' Jay said. 'Didn't he tell Bashta?'

'He didn't tell me!' Bertram said, frowning fiercely.

'Why would he?' Chris wanted to know. He was using a chunk of bread to mop up his gravy and wondering if he would be allowed seconds.

'Because I work there, I'm a supervisor you know!' Bertram sounded indignant.

'No you're not!' Jay said. 'Bashta is. You're the same as me, you work for him until you're told differently. You're not in Salutem now, you know.'

Bertram grunted but his face reddened. He stabbed viciously at his food with a fork.

'Have they asked you what you want to do when this job is finished?' Chris asked him, hoping to calm the situation.

Bertram shook his head. 'I think we're about done with the job though,' he said around a mouthful of food. He swallowed and took a mouthful of batu before continuing. 'Wonder if I'll get the tour you got with Anilla? I missed out on that.'

Chris wondered if Bertram had always sounded this petulant.

'I'd have thought you would want to be in the Smithcraft,' he said. 'Given your talents.'

Bertram looked at him. 'Have I ever met any of the smiths?' he asked.

'Of course you have! Bashta and Sam are both smiths,' Jay said. 'They do all the technical stuff round here. It's specialist work. That's where all the inventors seem to be too.'

'Hmm, that might suit me.' Bertram looked thoughtful as he continued his meal.

Anilla appeared and took a seat beside Jay. 'Good evening,' she said. 'Had a good day?'

'Brilliant!' Jay said. 'But tiring. How about you?'

'I had a lovely day, thank you,' she said, 'I hadn't realised I missed the bees so much.' She smiled happily, then focused her attention on Bertram. 'Bert, I've been asked to see you about your choice of occupation, as your job with Bashta is almost at an end.'

Bertram nodded. 'The lads were just asking me about that,' he said. 'But I've no idea, I didn't get the same tour Chris did.'

Anilla flushed at his accusatory tone. 'Fallaren has requested that you consider going into the smith crafters hall, he thinks you would do well there. They appreciate your inventiveness. But of course, it's up to you.'

'I dunno,' Bertram said gruffly. It was difficult to say no when the leader himself had suggested he work there. 'Can I go visit them and see what they do?'

'Of course,' Anilla said immediately. 'I'll arrange that for tomorrow morning, straight after breakfast. I'll let Bashta know, but I don't think he'll be surprised. Do you get on well with him?'

The question surprised Bertram, but he nodded. 'Yeah, he seems ok, knows his stuff. I'd say we get on well. Why?'

'As you probably know, he's from the smith hall and you'll still be working with him.

Bertram nodded and seemed pleased. He returned his attention to his meal as Anilla began talking to Jay and Chris.

'You enjoyed your day then?' she asked Jay. 'Garad speaks well of you. I'm so pleased you're working with them; they've needed more help for a long time, but they put folk off with their gruff ways.'

'Nah, they're fine,' Jay said. 'The work's fascinating, much better than fishing.' He pulled a face.

'Wait! You got to go work with the paper making guys?' Bertram was almost shouting now. 'How come he gets to go to such a prestigious profession and I'm being shunted off to the smiths?' he demanded.

Anilla looked cross. 'You're not being shunted off,' she said hotly. 'Your work with Bashta has shown you have talents, Fallaren feels you would be best placed within the smith hall.' She glared at Bertram, who dropped his gaze, a dull red flush rising on his cheeks. 'And what makes you think the smiths are less well thought of? I'm going now,' she stood up. 'I'll see you in the morning Bert.'

'Bye Anilla,' Chris and Jay chorused before turning on Bertram. 'You weren't very nice to her Bertram,' Chris said. 'She was only trying to help you, and the smiths obviously want you over with them. Why shout at her for something that's not her fault, she was only delivering a message, from the leader at that!'

'Yeah,' Jay chimed in, 'Anilla's lovely, she always tries to help everyone.'

Bertram merely huffed. 'She can't even get my name right.' He finished his food quickly and strode off, leaving his dirty plate and cup on the table.

Chris looked after him and shook his head. 'I think he's jealous,' he said at last.

Jay nodded. 'I reckon,' he said. 'He does keep going on about prestige doesn't he, and he can't stand the thought of you doing something 'better' than him.' He shook his head. 'Some friend. If you ask me, you'd be better off without him.'

Chris frowned, 'He's been my mate my whole life,' he said slowly. 'Back in Salutem he was part of the gang, up for fun and part of the planning to get out, just like me. He seems different here though and I can't figure out why.' He shook his head. 'Maybe going straight to work instead of getting the tour with me did him no favours.'

Jay looked doubtful. 'Maybe,' he said. 'Do you think he'll go for the smiths?'

'No idea,' Chris said. 'Like you said, he keeps going on about prestige, he might think they're beneath him. I hope Garad and Edwin don't take him on, that hut's not big enough.'

'Can't see it myself,' Jay said. 'They're not known for accepting others. You're the first for years, as I understand it. I was thinking though,' he paused, looking shyly at Chris. 'How about we see if we can get accommodation together? Just the two of us. If Bertie doesn't go to the smiths that is, cos if he does, he'll move over there with them.'

'Can we do that?' Chris asked, 'is there space? What about Seb?'

'We're not in the caves now,' Jay said. 'I know there's some empty places. Seb's been given rooms over near the hospital, they're trying to move all the healer types over there so they're all together for learning and whatnot,' he looked vague. 'I'm still not sure exactly what it is he does over there you know, and he's told me loads of times.' He laughed and swallowed the last of his Harbatu. 'Ugh, cold,' he said, grimacing.

Chris nodded. 'Yeah, if Bertram doesn't go to the smith hall, I think it would be great if you and I could share accommodation. Couldn't we just stay where we are though?'

'No, that's just temporary accommodation for newcomers,' Jay said. 'They were wanting to move Seb and me out when you two arrived and we got left there to help you guys out.'

Chris was thoughtful. 'Yeah, I think us sharing would be great,' he said. 'Hope they don't decide that we should all live in our crafting groups, don't fancy being cooped up with Garad and Edwin all the time.'

Jay looked pleased and began stacking dirty dishes, including Bertram's abandoned plate. 'Nah, they have families. Best get these done and find places, there's a telling tonight, at the big firepit,' he said.

Chris scrambled to help his friend and they made their way across to the firepit. There was already quite a crowd gathered but they managed to get onto one of the long benches only a couple of rows back.

'Tark and Merel are telling tonight,' Jay whispered.

'How do you know?' Chris asked. 'You've been with me all day.'

'Cos they're just walking up,' Jay grinned.

The crowd settled quickly as Merel and Tark took their seats by the fire and, as Merel stood, an expectant hush fell. She strummed on a lute and sang a song. It told of folk long ago, of the battle with the dragons and of how brave people tamed some of them instead of running and hiding.

Chris and Jay exchanged looks. 'Our ancestors were all for running and hiding apparently,' Jay whispered. Chris nodded, his attention on Merel.

After the song had ended there was huge applause and cheering and, flushing, Merel sat down. Tark stood and began the tale of the evening. As the firelight flickered, he told of a young girl who could spin and weave like no other, but her skills caught the attention of the wrong man and she was kidnapped. Then Tark told of her father's attempts at finding her, and of her own attempts at escape. Finally, her captor told her she could be free if only she would weave for him a fine wall hanging showing the great battle of the dragons. She agreed, even though the piece would likely take years to complete. Eventually, after ten long years, the hanging was done and the man kept his word and let her go back to her family, who held a great feast in celebration of her return. The final words of the story fell into the silence and, as Tark sat down, the applause began. Chris joined in enthusiastically, Jay whistling and clapping beside him.

'That was brilliant!' Chris said, as they made their way to their beds.

Jay nodded, stifling a yawn. 'I wonder,' he said sleepily, 'If all these stories and songs will get written down in books that we make?'

Chris shrugged. 'Wouldn't be a bad idea,' he said. 'But I really enjoyed listening to Tark and Merel. Wouldn't be the same reading it.'

They were still talking about it when they got home. They were met by Seb at the doorway who motioned them to be silent. Inside, Bertram was in bed but huffing and moving around a lot, obviously not asleep. The others ignored him and quietly got into their beds.

*****

The following morning Bertram seemed more like his old self and walked with Jay and Chris to get breakfast. They were sitting together devouring their sausages, eggs and bacon, when Anilla approached their table with an older man in tow.

'Bert,' she said. 'This is Ivan, he's one of the senior smith crafters. He's here to take you over to their hall so you can see what goes on. He'll guide you round so you can see if you think you'd like working with them.'

Bertram looked up into Ivan's face and, if he'd been about to argue, changed his mind. The man's face was set in a stern expression, his dark eyes upon Bertram. 'That's great,' he managed in a choked voice. 'I'm almost done, won't be a minute.'

Anilla looked up at Ivan, who nodded briefly at her, then she left. Chris and Jay exchanged worried looks and Jay turned to watch her go.

'Hope Anilla's alright,' he said. 'Not like her not to stop and chat for a bit.'

'She's busy.' Ivan said. His voice was deep and rough. 'As am I.'

Bertram gave the others a worried look before bolting the rest of his breakfast. 'I'll just take these back, then I'm ready,' he said, picking up his plate and still full mug. He drank the batu on the way to the cleaning station, Ivan following him. Bertram gave Chris and Jay a brief wave before turning to follow Ivan, who was striding away. Bertram was nearly running to keep up with him.

'Well!' Jay said, watching them leave, 'Looks like he's in for a fun day, doesn't it?'

'Hope it doesn't put him off the smiths altogether. From what I've heard, he'd be well suited there, he's clever you know.'

Jay nodded. 'Shame about his attitude.'

'I know,' Chris was collecting dishes together. 'Don't know what's up with him. C'mon, time to go.'

They collected their lunch bags from Scoria and hurried away.

Chapter 8 – A ray of hope

They didn't see Bertram for a few days, meanwhile Chris and Jay, who had now officially left the fishers and was a fully-fledged and pinned paper crafting apprentice, were learning fast what it was to be an apprentice in the paper crafters. Their fingers were shrivelled into ridges and their backs and shoulders were aching as they made their way home after work on the third day after Bertram left.

'What I need,' Jay said, 'is a good old soak at the bathhouse. Fancy it?'

'Yes!' Chris said. 'That would help the aches.' He eased his back as he dumped his empty lunch bag onto his bed.

'Never realised that making paper would be such hard work.' Jay said. 'I'm torn between bathing and sleeping.' He gave a half-hearted laugh.

'Bathing, definitely bathing.' Chris said with a groan.

They gathered their things and were leaving when they heard a shout. Turning, they saw Bertram trotting up the street towards them.

'Hey stranger.' Chris greeted him. 'How are things with the smiths?'

Bertram wrinkled his nose. 'Hot, noisy and smelly,' he said. 'Where are you two off to?'

'Bath house,' Jay said, 'speaking of smelly.'

'Mind if I join you?' Bertram asked.

'Feel free,' Chris said, ignoring Jay, who was standing behind Bertram, shaking his head.

Five minutes later they were all submerged in the warm waters.

'Oh that's better!' Jay closed his eyes with a sigh. 'My poor shoulders don't know what's hit 'em.'

'Paper making hard work, is it?' Bertram asked unsympathetically.

'Yup. Well, the bit of it we're doing is.' Chris replied. 'They've got us stripping bark from trees and pounding the insides up to make mush.'

'Sounds like...fun?' Bertram said. 'The smiths had me bashing huge stones with hammers so they could extract the ore. Then I was hefting stones into a huge oven thing, and then I had to learn how to work bellows properly. And man everyone over there shouts!'

'You're not keen then?' Jay asked dreamily, floating in the deep water.

'Not really,' Bertram said. 'I was hoping to get to know more about other crafts before I make a final decision, but to be honest, I've not seen much over there that makes me want to stay.'

'You're going to get the mucky jobs wherever you go,' Jay said, 'learn from the bottom up and all that.'

'But I have experience,' Bertram said indignantly.

'Then you'll probably work your way up faster than most,' Jay said reasonably. 'Better to know all about your craft, rather than just bits, don't you think?'

It sounded perfectly reasonable to Chris. 'Yeah, I

mean, we're pounding trees to smithereens at the moment, but at some point Garad is going to show us what to do with it and we'll be able to learn more technical stuff. I'm sure the smiths will be the same.'

Jay nodded, standing up in the middle of the pool, water sheeting off his hair. 'He was on about using hemp, wasn't he? They're full of ideas, that pair.'

Bertram was under water now, bubbles rising around him. Chris and Jay shared a look, and Jay mouthed 'I hope he doesn't decide he wants to join us!'

Chris grinned; he could imagine Garad's response to Bertram's attitude.

Once they had bathed and dressed, the three made their way to the main dining area for their evening meal. The tables were already busy and their usual spot was taken. They stood, trays laden, looking for a space. Chris spotted Anilla waving at them.

'Look, over there, Anilla's got a table,' he said to the others and began weaving his way between diners. 'Busy tonight,' he said by way of greeting as he sat next to Anilla.

'Hello, how was your day?' Anilla asked pointedly.

'Sorry,' Chris grinned unrepentantly. 'Hi Anilla, how are you? How was your day? Jay and I think Garad's trying to kill us.'

'I'm alright,' she began, 'he's what? What's he doing to you?'

'Nothing really,' Jay was chuckling as he took the seat opposite Chris. 'It's just hard, heavy work and we weren't expecting it. It'll get better as we go onto the more technical stuff, I'm sure.'

Anilla looked relieved. 'So you're both alright over there?' she asked, 'they're being nice to you?'

'Nice?' a frown wrinkled Jay's brow, 'they're ok with us.'

'They're fine.' Chris said. 'They've been a pair for so long it must be hard for them to have us there with them, even though they asked for me,' he said thoughtfully. 'But we're learning how to get along with one another, and it's interesting over there. I can't wait to learn how to make books.'

Bertram had listened to this while making a start on his meal. 'I need to talk to whoever organises the work details,' he said abruptly, wiping gravy from his chin.

All eyes turned to him. 'That's usually my job, Bert. Do you have a problem?' Anilla said.

'Yeah, I think so,' he said. 'I'm not happy with what I'm being asked to do. They've got me breaking rocks for heaven's sake!'

'I assume it's work that needs doing,' Anilla said, 'and it's usually the newcomers that get that type of work I'm afraid.'

'Yeah, well,' Bertram sounded sulky and Chris and Jay glanced at each other. Anilla caught the look but said nothing. 'I want to know more about other jobs before I make a decision. I have experience you know, I was a supervisor in Salutem, it's not right that I have to start at the bottom again.'

'It's a shame you don't feel the smith craft is right for you,' Anilla said gently, 'I've had good reports from the masters over there. They say you're strong and a hard worker, and you seem keen to learn. Hmm, well, I shall have a word with Fallaren and Narilka and see if they have any recommendations. Someone with your skills must be allowed to use them in a productive way.'

Bertram seemed calmer after her speech and returned his attention to his meal.

'Is there anything happening tonight?' Chris asked, trying to ease the tension around the table.

'I don't think so,' Anilla said. 'No doubt there'll be folk playing instruments and some singing, there usually is, but no storytelling as there was the other night. Did you enjoy it?'

'It was brilliant!' Chris said, more eagerly than he'd planned. 'We used to have entertainments back in Salutem, but only really once a month, and nothing like that. I suspect there's no subliminal messaging in Portum for a start.'

'What?' Anilla and Jay looked startled. Bertram glanced at Chris and gave him a twisted half smile.

'It's really why we were so keen on leaving,' Chris said. 'We found out about their subliminals, keeping everyone subdued and quelling curiosity about the outside world. We thought we could get outside, see for ourselves what the truth was and then get back in and tell everyone, prove they were lying.'

Bertram snorted quietly then, having finished his meal, stood up. 'I'm going to bed,' he announced. 'Should I look for you after breakfast Anilla?'

'I think you should have tomorrow with the

smiths,' Anilla said, still obviously shaken by Chris' revelation. 'Fallaren and Narilka are busy this evening. I'll try to find them in the morning and discuss your options with them.'

'Huh, fine.' Bertram grabbed his tray and stomped off.

'What has got into him?' Anilla wanted to know. 'You'd think, given what you just told us Chris, that he'd be so glad to be out of Salutem that he'd be happy with just about any occupation so he can breathe fresh air and see the daylight.'

Chris was shaking his head, frowning as he watched Bertram leave. 'No idea,' he said, 'although he does still seem obsessed with rank. It all goes back to Salutem and his father. Daddy wanted him to get a ranking job, wouldn't let him pair with the girl he said he wanted because she wasn't high enough in the society for his liking.' He looked sad. 'Bertram was always in the gang though; he and I engineered the escape together. He was fighting against his father and the other leaders so we could discover the truth. Then he goes all weird when we finally get out.'

'Still!' Jay said with feeling. 'There's no need to be rude, or to act like a sulky toddler. Anilla, I've been meaning to ask, if he doesn't go to the smith hall permanently, is there any chance Chris and me could have somewhere else to live? He's not easy company, always grumping and huffing.'

'It's about time you had proper, permanent accommodation,' she said, 'I know there are a couple of places vacant.'

'Yeah,' Jay nodded, 'I saw there's one at the edge, near the river, closer to work for us. We wouldn't have so far to walk before we can collapse on an evening.' He gave a half smile, looking with concern at his unusually quiet friend.

The three of them sat at the table together long after the other diners had left, talking about their experiences of Portum and of their previous lives. The moon was up when they said good night and made their way back to their sleeping quarters.

***

The next morning Bertram managed to wake them both up by banging around as he got ready for his day with the smiths.

'Bertram!' Chris yawned widely. 'Did you have to bump into me like that?'

Bertram huffed. 'Well, I've got to be up!'

'We don't!' Jay said from the other bunk, 'and our work's hard going too you know!'

'Oh dear, how sad.' Bertram left the hut and they could hear him stomping up the street for his breakfast.

'He should have stayed over at the smith hall last night, then he wouldn't have to be up so early,' Jay said, pulling the covers over his shoulders and trying to get comfortable again.

'He should,' sighed Chris, shaking his head sadly. He sat up on the edge of his bed. 'I may as well get up,' he said. 'I'm wide awake now.'

Jay lay in bed a minute or two longer while Chris got himself washed and dressed, then he got up too.

'Wonder if Anilla will be able to find him a different job?' he said, his voice muffled by the towel he was using to dry his face.

'Hope so,' Chris said. He finished making his bed and pulled the curtains back to let the early morning light in. 'If she does, maybe he'll cheer up a bit. You know, sometimes I find myself wishing he'd stayed in Salutem. Daddy would have made sure he got a top job there.' He sounded bitter.

Jay gave him a grin, 'I'd rather be out here, getting burned by the sun and learning to make paper with you, than stuck in those dull, dreary caves with no hopes of a decent life.'

'Me too!' Chris gave his friend a determined smile, 'early breakfast? Let's see if we can beat Garad and Edwin to work, shall we?'

***

Bertram was finishing his breakfast by the time they got to the dining area. Chris gave him a cheery wave as he and Jay went to get their breakfasts. When they had filled their plates and turned to go and take seats, he had left.

'I can't pretend to be disappointed, but how rude!' Jay said.

'Yup,' Chris said sadly, taking a seat at the nearest table. 'Enough about him, let's eat!'

They finished their meals and Jay found Scoria for their lunch bags while Chris took the plates for cleaning.

They were halfway to the river when they heard a shout behind them. Turning they saw Garad and Edwin waving at them. Chris grinned. 'We almost made it,' he said quietly as they waited for the older men to catch them up.

'You two are early this morning,' Edwin said.

'Eager, they are.' Garad was smiling. 'Good to see.'

They walked together and Garad told them about his plans to expand their workplace. 'Talked to Fallaren last night,' he said. 'He thinks it's a grand idea, give us more space, especially now we've got you two young 'uns.'

'Would mean we can up production,' Edwin chimed in cheerfully.

Chris and Jay looked at each other and burst out laughing.

'What's up with you two?' Garad wanted to know.

'I thought you didn't want anyone joining you.' Chris said. 'That's what Anilla told me. Now suddenly you're on about expanding and everything.'

'Ah, well, Fallaren and Narilka seem very keen that we do more,' Garad told them. 'Seems our paper is in demand by other villages. If we have more, we can trade more. They seem to like you two lads too.' He was nodding, smiling. 'It's good to feel we're important to the village.'

'You always were,' Chris said. 'Anilla told me that when she was showing me round on my first day here.'

'And here's me thinking we was just a pair of old nuisances, turning out a couple of books now and then.' Edwin teased his friend.

'Yeah, well, we probably were,' Garad said, rubbing his beard, 'but now, now we're in business. We got ourselves a couple of apprentices and the paper crafters are going places!'

'We are.' Jay said, chuckling, 'we're going all the way over there.' He pointed to the building they worked in.

Laughing, they crossed the bridge and went to make a start on their day.

***

It was late evening. Chris and Jay were sitting around the firepit enjoying the singing with Garad and Edwin, when Bertram appeared. He was covered in soot and dust and he looked annoyed.

'Hey,' he grabbed Chris by the arm and pulled at him. 'Where's your little friend?'

'Get off me!' Chris pulled his arm away, astonished by Bertram's appearance and behaviour. 'Which friend do you mean?' he asked, although he had a fair idea.

'The girl, the one who's supposed to be finding me decent work.' Bertram's temper was clearly very short this evening.

'I don't know,' Chris said calmly, 'we haven't seen her today at all.'

'Huh.' Without invitation, Bertram sat next to them and glowered around at the folk of Portum who, after a few curious looks in his direction, returned to their group singing.

Chris and Jay exchanged looks before continuing singing. Garad had proved to have a surprisingly good voice, Edwin less so, but they had joined in heartily, encouraging their young co-workers to do the same. Beside them, Bertram huffed and groaned, but no one took any notice of him, until Garad turned to him.

'Young fella, I don't know what's up, but if you're gonna sit there huffing like a broken bellows, take yoursen somewhere else to do it.'

Bertram could hardly believe his ears. 'Don't you know who I am?' he said. 'Don't you know who my father is? Is there no respect given to anyone in this place?' He stood up and glowered, deliberately leaning over Garad.

Garad stood up, he was a good foot taller and much broader than Bertram. 'No, I don't,' he said quietly and his voice held an edge of menace, 'and I don't much care. What happened in Salutem, stays in Salutem as far as I'm concerned.'

'I am the son of the next leader!' Bertram said, puffing out his chest.

'Not out here you're not.'

Bertram took a deep breath, saw the look on Garad's face and thought better of it. Instead, he turned his back on him and stormed off.

'What's got into your mate?' Garad asked. 'Was he always like this?'

'No,' Chris looked glum, 'he doesn't seem to like it much in Portum.'

'Happen he wishes he was back in them caves,' Edwin said, 'he seems to want to be like his Daddy.' He wrinkled his nose in distaste. 'Looks like we're done for the night. See ya tomorrow morning lads,' He and Garad rose and strode away together, leaving Chris and Jay to wander reluctantly towards their home. As they passed the council rooms a door flew open and Anilla popped her head out.

'Hey,' she said in a loud whisper, 'in here!'

Looking at one another in surprise, Chris and Jay entered the building.

'What's up?' Jay asked, looking around in disbelief at the leaders and a few of the crafting masters who were gathered in the room around the huge, heavy wooden table.

'We're trying to decide on options for your friend,' Fallaren said. His voice sounded strained and he looked weary.

'Ah,' Chris glanced at Anilla, 'having trouble?'

'Just a little,' she replied.

'We're alright with him staying with us,' the man Chris remembered from the smith hall said. He was huge, taking up all the space between himself and his neighbours with his broad shoulders and arms. 'But he doesn't seem to want to. He's all about being in charge, that lad. Has a few lessons to learn if you ask me.'

'We were hoping,' Fallaren said to Chris, 'that you may be able to give us some clues so we can help Bert find his feet here in Portum.'

The assembled masters looked hopefully at Chris, who flushed at finding himself the centre of attention. He cleared his throat.

'Well,' he began, 'as you probably know, his father is Commander Tolson's Chief of Staff, so Bertram always had certain…privileges back in Salutem. He had status I suppose, in our group of friends, when I came up with ideas he tried to claim them as his own. I guess that's why he was desperate to get out with me, so that I couldn't say I did it and he didn't.'

'But you did get out,' Narilka spoke, 'and you, Chris, are settling in here, you're making friends and adjusting to the outside world well. Bert, unfortunately, doesn't seem to be adapting at all. We're not interested in status here, he needs to understand that before we can move forward with him,' she frowned, 'and we had such high hopes for the pair of you too. Bert's a strong lad, he would make a great dragon rider, if only he would pull himself together.'

'Maybe you should tell him that.' Chris suggested. 'It may make the difference to him.'

Narilka shook her head slightly. 'We can offer no guarantees,' she said.

'I'll have a word with him, if you like,' Chris said, suspecting that the chance of the prestige of becoming a dragon rider might be enough to turn Bertram around.

'Thank you.' Narilka nodded at him before returning her attention to the meeting they had interrupted.

'Thank you,' Anilla whispered, 'I hope Bert comes round, I'm certain he could do well in Portum.'

'I'll see what I can do,' Chris said quietly, 'come on Jay, let's go.'

Jay nodded and together they made their way home.

***

Bertram was still up when they arrived, freshly washed and changed, he scowled at them when they walked in.

Chris spoke immediately, before Bertram had the chance to start shouting at them again. 'We've just seen Anilla,' he said.

Bertram, who had been drawing breath to complain again, paused. 'And?'

'And she was in a meeting with Fallaren, Narilka and a load of the craft masters,' Chris told him. 'They were trying to sort out work for you that would use your skill set.'

Bertram nodded, his eyes never leaving Chris' face. 'Go on.'

'Narilka said something,' Chris sighed. 'She said that they had high hopes for you here in Portum,' he paused, 'they were hoping, if you settle in well, that you might become a dragon rider.'

The change in Bertram was instantaneous. His eyes lit up and the sullen look left his face. 'Really?'

Chris and Jay nodded. 'That's what she said,' Jay agreed, 'and no one looked surprised, so they must all feel that way. That big smith chap, he said they'd like you to stay working with them too.'

Bertram nodded. 'But riders care for their dragons first, don't they?' he asked, 'I wouldn't have to be in the smith hall all the time?'

Chris nodded. 'That's how I understand it,' he said, 'Anilla told me that riders work in the afternoons, but most of the time they're taking care of the dragons, especially when they're young. Then it's training after that, learning how to fly, how to fight. You know. It's important work, they keep us all safe don't they.'

Bertram was silent, his eyes glittering.

'Anyway, I'm sure they'll be having a chat with you tomorrow,' Chris went on, 'but listen, don't say anything about being a rider, ok? Narilka said you'd have to show you were settling properly in Portum before you could be allowed to have a dragon.'

'I can do that,' Bertram said, squaring his shoulders. 'I can carry on with the smiths if I know it's not going to be forever. I do think my skills and ingenuity will be better appreciated over there.'

'I reckon you're right,' Jay said, trying to hide his smile, 'but you'll have to learn to do things their way first. I guess it's just a matter of local customs, they don't think you're useless or anything, or they wouldn't all have been in that room talking about you. It's just that they want you to learn Portum's ways.'

'Gotta walk before you run you know.' Chris chimed in, grinning at Bertram. 'I like it here bro,' he said, 'I really like it here. No one following us or listening in to what we're saying. Freedom to choose our work...our thoughts...' His voice tailed off.

Bertram returned his grin. 'I could have a dragon,' he said. 'I'll show them I can do it! Come on you two, bedtime, long day tomorrow, I've to be up early. Think I'll stop at the hall from now on though, makes sense, don't you think? You be alright here without me bro?'

'I'll be ok,' Chris said. 'I'm getting used to the place, and I have Jay, and work. And it's not like I'll never see you.'

'Good! Night then.' Bertram got into bed and turned his back on them.

Chris and Jay shared a triumphant grin before quietly readying themselves for bed.

Bertram was gone before they woke the next morning.

Anilla met them at breakfast. 'I don't know what you said to your friend,' she said, sitting next to Chris as he ate, 'but he was all smiles this morning and ready to go to work at the smith hall. He had his pack of belongings and everything.' She smiled at Chris, who glanced uneasily at Jay. 'I won't ask,' she said, her eyes twinkling, 'but I am glad he's changed his tune.'

She stayed with Chris while Jay went to get their lunches and gave his arm a little squeeze. 'Well done,' she whispered. 'Narilka and Fallaren were delighted at the change in Bert this morning. Now they think you're some kind of miracle worker.' She laughed at his stunned expression, 'Oh yes my friend, you are getting all the credit. They like you, you know.'

'Good,' Chris managed to say, but his voice wasn't much more than a squeak. He cleared his throat, 'I mean, good!' He made his voice as deep as he could, which made her laugh.

'Go on, get to work. I'll see you this evening I've no doubt.' She patted his arm and left, heading towards a table at which Fallaren and Narilka were seated, watching them.

Chapter 9 – A place to call home

'Garad, why are you making us do this?' Jay asked wearily, pushing his hair out of his eyes with his forearm. They were lifting soaking wood pulp from a large tub and spreading it, as thinly and evenly as possible into mesh lined wooden frames.

'All part of the job lad,' Garad said, 'an' until you knows how to do this properly, you're not ready for the next stage.'

'But it's been over a week now,' Jay said, trying not to moan. 'The same thing, every day.' He sagged onto the edge of the tub.

'I know,' Edwin said, without a shred of sympathy, 'but it's for your craft requirement.'

Chris and Jay looked enquiringly at him. 'Our what?' Chris said.

'Your craft requirement,' Garad sighed, 'I did tell you.'

Both boys shook their heads.

'You have to make a book, from start to finish,' Garad told them patiently, 'to get your journeyman pin. You know what that is doncha?'

Chris and Jay nodded mutely. They had endured a lengthy lecture about pins from Garad when he had presented them both with their apprentice pins. Chris was very proud of his. He glanced at it as it glinted on his left shoulder. The background was in the shape of a partly unrolled scroll, this was made of dull metal. Set in the centre was a polished white stone which Garad told him was quartz, an ore which was plentiful around Portum.

'Everyone needs to meet their crafting requirements,' Garad continued patiently. 'The tellers have to make an instrument, the fishers must craft a pot, and you two have to make a book, from start to finish, lettering, binding, the lot. You use that book as your record of your journey through the craft, it's yours, you copy all your notes in it as you go through processes and experiments.'

'You are making notes, aren't you?' Edwin interjected.

Chris and Jay looked guiltily at each other.

'That's the only way you'll know your craft inside out and that's how you become a journeyman.' Garad continued. 'Then, when you know enough of the basics, we can start experimenting with other materials. Need to get the basics done first though.'

'How long does it take?' Jay asked, hoping to encourage Garad to talk so they could have a rest.

'Normally at least three years,' Edwin said, 'sometimes longer. You have to show you know your craft thoroughly before you can progress.'

'The different stones mark ranks in the craft, don't they?' Chris put in.

'They do lad. Mine is an emerald,' Garad said, pointing unnecessarily at his pin, 'an' that means I'm a craft master. Edwin's is a sapphire, means he's..'

'Put upon and yelled at,' Edwin chipped in, grinning at the boys, who chuckled.

''Which means he's a journeyman,' Garad shook

his head at his friend. 'Means he can travel to other settlements to teach if he chooses. An' your pins are white quartz, means you're apprentices. The Craft Master, the leader of our craft, he wears a ruby pin.'

Chris looked at the pins, nodding. 'And we can be journeyman, can we? Like Edwin?'

'That you can lad, that you can. Folk are crying out for our paper, so it might be a good thing, give you both a taste of the world after being stuck in them caves for so long.'

Chris and Jay exchanged looks. Portum was quite enough world for the time being.

'Now, get on with what you're supposed to be doing,' Garad said sternly, 'or you'll not get beyond apprentice.'

Suppressing groans, they returned to their work.

***

That evening, for the first time since their conversation about becoming riders, Bertram appeared for the evening meal. He made his way over to where Chris and Jay were seated and clapped Chris on the back.

'Bro!' he exclaimed, a big grin on his face, 'miss me?' He put his bowl on the table and sat next to Chris.

'Bertram!' Chris sounded pleased to see his old friend. 'You're in a good mood. Suiting you over at the smiths, is it?' He took in Bertram's changed appearance. 'What happened to your hair?'

'Well, you know,' Bertram shrugged, running a hand over his now closely cropped hair. 'It's not so bad I suppose, hair had to go bro, too hot and mucky over there, and it's all in a good cause, if ya know what I mean.' He nudged Chris with his elbow and winked.

Jay and Chris glanced at each other, praying no one would overhear. 'You know I wasn't supposed to tell you about that,' Chris hissed. 'You've not said anything to anyone, have you?'

'Course not,' Bertram mumbled, busily eating his stew, 'but knowing that's what the plan is don't half help when I'm stuck doing the boring jobs.'

'We're the same,' Jay said, 'doing the boring jobs I mean,' he added hurriedly when Bertram looked quizzically at him. 'We've spent more than a week now just dumping soggy wet wood pulp into frames and smoothing it down, then we put it over a tub to drain, get some more soggy pulp. You get the picture.'

Bertram didn't look sympathetic. 'Have they asked you which area you want to specialise in yet?' He asked, taking a gulp of batu before adding, 'I'm interested in the hydro power plant they're building, it's really interesting stuff, actually making electricity from running water! The smiths are really progressive you know, inventing things all the time.' His face lit up and he prepared to tell them all about it.

Chris groaned inwardly; he knew that look. 'Glad you're happier in your work,' he said quickly, 'The paper craft isn't big enough for us to specialise the way you'll be able to in the smiths. We have to know everything about everything. It's going to take a while! Wonder when the hatching will be,' he added, almost too casually.

'Can't be long now,' Jay said. 'Eggs were laid just before you two arrived here, so maybe in the next couple of weeks?'

'I'm looking forward to it,' Chris said. 'Be interesting to see what happens, Anilla was very excited about it.'

Jay nodded, 'I've only seen one before,' he said, 'but it was great, and a brilliant party afterwards.' He was grinning now. 'That was the first time I saw Seb drunk,' he added, 'he was so funny, kept falling over and talking all slurred, telling me how much he loved me.' He was laughing now, shaking his head at the memory.

'Where is Seb?' Bertram asked.

'Healer hall,' Jay replied, 'he's living over there now.'

'Are you coming to the telling tonight?' Chris asked Bertram. 'It's a couple of the Journeymen I think, and some girl healer apprentice is going to sing.'

Bertram nodded. 'That's really why I'm here,' he said. 'A few of us came over this evening so we can listen.'

'Oh, not so you could see me then!' Chris looked at him in mock dismay.

'Why would I want to see you?' Bertram grinned giving Chris a nudge that almost sent him flying.

'Oh, I dunno, cos you're supposed to be my mate?' Chris was laughing. 'Seriously though bro, it's good to see you so happy.'

'You too, bro,' Bertram said. 'It's taken a little while, but I think I'm settling in here. I think the pair of us will do well in Portum, don't you?'

Chris was thoughtful. 'Yes,' he said, 'I can't see us ever going back to Salutem, can you? I'd miss the fresh air and sunshine.'

'Me too, not to mention old Tolson would have our guts for garters if we tried casually wandering back in. Can you picture it? *Oh, hi everyone, remember us? We just had a little adventure outside, it's really great, you should try it!*' He was grinning broadly now, 'Tolson would have a fit, he'd have the guards on us before we got the first sentence out. Not even my dad would be able to help us out, if he'd even acknowledge us that is.'

Chris was laughing, picturing the chaos such a scene would cause in Salutem. 'We'd be in the deep caves for a very long time. Good job we've no plans for returning really, isn't it?'

'Indeed,' said a voice behind them. They jumped and turned to see Fallaren and Narilka.

'Good evening,' Chris managed.

'Good evening to you too, Chris,' said Fallaren, slipping onto the bench next to Jay, who went bright pink.

'You boys seem to be enjoying yourselves,' Narilka said, 'good to see you've settled in.'

'Oh we have!' Bertram said emphatically.

'Bertie's in danger of getting sucked into the hydro-electric thing,' Jay said.

'Not sure that's how it works.' Fallaren laughed. His deep voice carried and folk at the nearby tables were turning to look at them.

Narilka put her hand on Chris' shoulder. 'We've been hearing good things about you, all of you, and we couldn't be happier. It's always good to hear that new people are settling in well and happy in their work, making friends. You're liking working with Garad and

Edwin?' She was looking at Jay now.

'Yes,' he said, 'I think they're trying to kill us, but I love learning about it all.'

'I'll let them know that death of apprentices is frowned on!' Fallaren was laughing loudly now, drawing yet more attention to their table.

'We must go and take our seats,' Narilka said to him. Still laughing he stood up. 'No doubt we will see you soon boys,' she smiled at them and left, Fallaren following her, calling out to several folk as he passed.

'That was...interesting,' Jay said after a moment. 'Never had that before. I mean, he was sat right next to me!'

'They do seem to like us, don't they,' Bertram said. 'Good, must mean they see something in us. Right, I'm off to find my mates and get seats for this thing tonight. See you over there.' He strode off towards a rowdy table near the edge of the dining area where he was greeted enthusiastically.

Chris, feeling overwhelmed by all the attention, sat staring silently at his empty plate.

'You ok?' Jay asked him.

'Yeah, I think so.' Chris was shaking his head. 'It was just a bit strange; don't you think? Fallaren and Narilka turning up like that, saying what they said. I'm sure they don't do that for all the newcomers, they'd never get a moment to themselves.'

'True,' Jay said, 'perhaps Bertie's right, that they see something in us? Hey,' he grinned, 'we're the future of Portum!'

Chris snorted. 'Come on,' he said, 'let's go get seats, they'll be starting soon.'

They found places near the back of the crowd and settled themselves as comfortably as they could on the wooden bench. One of the tellers stood up and the crowd fell silent.

The tale was only part way through when Chris felt a nudge in his back. He turned to see Anilla beckoning to him.

'You two, come with me,' she whispered.

Puzzled, the boys crept away from the listening crowd and followed her towards the council hall.

'What's going on?' Chris asked as soon as he could speak without disturbing the telling.

'Remember asking me about new living accommodation?' Anilla asked. They nodded. 'Well, you have been assigned somewhere to live. This will be your permanent home, at least until you get paired, or become riders or whatever.'

'Do we really need it?' Chris queried. 'Now that Bertram's gone over to the smiths full time?'

'Yes.' Anilla sounded firm. 'You need permanent accommodation so you feel more settled. And we need your current spot for more incomers. We've just received word that four more are being brought in tomorrow.'

'Excellent!' Jay sounded excited. 'Where is it?'

'Hold on,' Chris said, as his brain caught up with what Anilla had said. 'Until we become riders? Where did that come from?'

'Fallaren and Narilka,' Anilla said, almost squeaking with delight. 'They said they want me to stand. Not at this hatching obviously, but maybe next time.'

'Anilla, that's great!' Jay was grinning from ear to ear.

Without thinking, Chris put his arms around her and gave her a big hug. She looked surprised but allowed the hug to continue. He let her go, holding her by the shoulders. 'I'm so pleased for you,' he said, 'you're obviously thrilled. Riding does run in the family, doesn't it!' A thought struck him. 'Are Narilka and Fallaren riders?'

'Yes, it's usual for our leaders to be riders too.' Anilla told him. 'Being a rider means you have good leadership qualities. They must be strong and clear headed and good at managing many different things at the same time.' She spoke as if reciting something she'd learned in school. 'And Fallaren and Narilka are popular with everyone too, which helps.'

Jay was nodding. 'Yes, yes, fascinating,' he said, 'but what about our new home?'

Anilla turned towards the huge table which dominated the centre of the hall. Papers and scrolls were strewn across it. She flicked through a couple before locating the sheet she was looking for.

'Here it is.' She said. 'You have been allocated house number 16, it's at the edge of the main village settlement, near the river. Remember Jay, you noticed it before and mentioned it to me?'

Jay nodded vigorously. 'I remember,' he said, 'I reckon it's perfect. I had a good look through the windows the other week. It'll need some work mind, but it's nothing we can't do ourselves…or persuade others to do for us.' His grin took on an evil glint.

'You'll be needing this,' Anilla held out a smaller sheet of stiff paper. 'You have to sign it, then you keep it in the cottage, in the holder by the door, you know how it works Jay?'

'Yeah, I get it,' he replied, already placing it on the table and looking for a writing implement. Anilla handed him a pen. He signed and held it out to Chris, pointing to where he needed to sign.

'What's this for then?' Chris asked.

'This proves that the house is yours,' Anilla told him. 'It is already logged in our records as yours, but this, kept by the door, means no one can come along and say you've no right to be there, or claim it for themselves. We brought this in after a couple of ugly incidents where folk decided a house was worth fighting over.'

'When can we move in?' Jay interrupted. He could hardly stand still.

'Immediately, if you like,' Anilla was laughing at him, 'you're certainly keen.'

'I am,' Jay said, 'I can't stand those bunks, be nice to sleep in a proper bed.'

'Well, I've had clean sheets and blankets sent over for you,' Anilla said, 'so you just need to go get your things from your old place and get yourselves settled in your new home.'

'Thank you Anilla,' Chris said, quietly. 'You've done so much for us, for me…since I got here and I really appreciate it.'

Anilla blushed, 'I'm happy to help you,' she said quietly, 'I like helping new folk to settle in, and you two are some of the nicest we've had in a long while.'

'We're fabulous,' Jay put in, 'now come on mate, we've got moving in to do!'

With a last smile of thanks to Anilla, the boys left and jogged up the street to their bunk house. It didn't take them long to gather their belongings and they were soon on the way to their new home.

'Good job you know where it is Jay,' Chris said, panting slightly as he hurried to keep up with his friend.

'I did point it out to you,' Jay said, grinning back over his shoulder, 'come on, keep up!' He broke into a trot.

'Hey, wait!' Chris ran after him and a couple of minutes later they arrived, panting, at their home.

Number 16 was larger than their old bunk house, there was a small kitchen, a proper dining table with stools set under it, and a comfortable seating area. The cushions on these seats matched the curtains, which were faded dark green and yellow.

'I think we'll need to sweet talk someone into making us some new curtains and stuff,' Jay said, strolling around the room.

Chris, who was sliding the paper Anilla had given them into its holder by the door, looked over his shoulder, 'Yes,' he said firmly, 'those are awful! Do we know who was living in here before us?'

'Not a clue, it's been empty since I got here,' Jay shrugged. 'But who cares? It's ours now!' Gleefully, he threw himself down onto the couch and stretched out, one arm cushioning his head. 'Aah,' he sighed, 'this is the life!'

Chris looked around. 'It's a nice place,' he said, 'bigger at least. What's through here?' He opened one of the two doors on the back wall. It revealed a small bedroom which held bed and a cupboard. The second door opened into a similar room. As Anilla had promised, there was a pile of fresh linens and towels on each bed.

'Gonna need new throws too, these are a bit flowery, aren't they,' Jay said, 'but at least it's all nice and clean.'

'Where do we get washed?' Chris wondered, wandering back into the main room.

'There's usually a special little room,' Jay said, looking round, 'but we don't appear to have one. How strange.' He went outside and walked right round the house.

Chris stalked around the main room, frowning slightly and thinking, then he went into one of the bedrooms and looked around. He was back in the main room, grinning, when Jay came back in.

'What're you grinning at?'

'Found it.' Chris announced.

'Where?'

Chris beckoned, 'in here,' he led Jay into the bedroom and pointed to a door in the wall which they hadn't noticed the door on their brief inspection. Chris opened it with a flourish, and ushered Jay through into a tiny room. It held a washstand with a large metal jug, used for fetching the water, and, in the corner, stood a covered bucket. A wooden rack next to the washstand already held two clean towels and wash cloths.

'Nice,' Jay said, 'we'll just have to make sure we don't both open the doors at the same time,' he said, 'or we'll knock one another out!'

'If this hydroelectric thing that Bertram's banging on about gets going, we might even have running water.' Chris said, closing the door as they left their tiny bathing room. 'I do miss running water.'

They chose bedrooms and swiftly unpacked.

Chris left his room to find Jay looking interestedly at the kitchen area. He looked up as Chris approached. 'Do you know how to cook?' he asked.

'Me? No,' Chris laughed, 'weren't allowed in Salutem, we were all herded to the dining room and the kitchen folk served us our measured portions of whatever glop they'd thought up for the day. What about you?'

'Same,' Jay said, 'Barlang wasn't quite as bad as Salutem sounds, but we weren't taught how to cook, or wash clothes or anything, it was someone's job and why would we ever need to know that kind of thing? We were in there for life, it's worse than bloody prison!'

Chris nodded, 'I know, but hey,' he patted Jay's arm soothingly, 'we're out now, we're here, breathing fresh air, learning to make paper and books. We have our own space! I've never had a bedroom of my own, well, any space of my own.'

Jay nodded but he looked miserable. 'I hated those caves,' he began.

'But you miss the people?' Chris suggested.

'Yeah,' Jay sighed, 'I know Seb's here with me, for

what that's worth cos I never see him now, but I miss my mates, my parents. You understand, don't you?'

'Of course I do, and I never thought I would miss them like I do. My friends were thrown in the deep caves for daring to think about escape. Bertram and I were the lucky ones, we made it out.'

'How did you manage it? I mean if they caught the others...'

'We weren't where we were supposed to be,' Chris said, 'they'd have looked for us, but we were already away, running through tunnels on the way to find out if the outside world even existed.' He shook his head. 'Seems amazing to me now that they want to keep people holed up in those caves, living such restricted, small lives. I mean, they must know what it's like out here, why not let folk outside to live properly?'

'No idea mate,' Jay said sadly, 'it's cruel really. Shame we can't go back and tell everyone the truth.'

Chris agreed and they both sank into the cushioned seats, looking and feeling sadder than they had since coming to Portum. A knock at the door startled them and Jay roused himself sufficiently to bid their visitor to come in.

Anilla poked her head round the door, smiling brightly at them both. 'I just thought I'd come and see how my favourites are settling in,' she said, glancing worriedly from one sad face to the other. 'And I can see you're both...looking absolutely miserable! What's the matter? Don't you like your cottage?'

'The cottage is fine, thanks for arranging it for us,' Chris managed to speak, although his throat felt tight and dry. 'We just got talking about the caves we came from, and our families and friends and how we miss them...' his voice trailed off and tears filled his eyes.

'It's knowing we'll never see them again,' Jay added, 'knowing that they're all stuck in there, and we're out here, loving our new lives. I wish we could go rescue them all, but I know we can't,' he finished on a sigh.

'No, you can't I'm afraid,' Anilla said briskly, 'but you can make the best of it now that you're here, and up to this evening I truly thought you were!'

'We are!' Chris declared, 'we just miss people, that's all. It's Jay's fault,' he continued, starting to cheer up a little.

'My fault?'

'Yeah, you asked if I could cook,'

Anilla looked confused. 'He asked if you could cook and that led to this?' She waved a hand at the pair of them. 'I walk in here to find you two miserable and longing for your old homes? Advice, don't cook if it makes you this sad!'

'But we have this lovely kitchen,' Chris said, the beginnings of a smile played around his mouth. Funny how she always made him feel better.

'I bet you'd burn water,' Anilla teased, 'best leave it to those who know what they're doing, at least for now. However, you can always make yourselves some batu, you have a pot look.' She opened the oven door and removed a metal pot with a lid. 'You put fresh water in here,' she removed the lid to demonstrate, 'and when it's boiling,' catching their blank looks she clarified, 'when there's lots of steam coming out of the spout, you take it off the stove, but be careful, it'll be very hot, and put the leaves in. Leave it for a few minutes and, hey presto, freshly made batu.'

Chris was shaking his head. 'Did you understand that Jay?' he asked.

'Nope,' Jay said, 'I could understand the individual words, of course I could, but all together? Made no sense to me at all.' He grinned at Anilla who shook her head at him.

'Well, I'm glad you're both feeling better,' she said, 'even if it means teasing me.'

After she'd left them, the boys sat talking for a long time, relishing having their own home.

'I still can't quite get over how free we are here,' Chris said. 'In Salutem everything was controlled, everything, down to how much we could eat. And privacy?' he laughed. 'It just didn't exist, unless you were one of the leaders of course, but the rest of us couldn't even bathe in private.'

'It's the same where I'm from,' Jay said. 'We were told what work we were going to do, where we would live, how we would live, and obviously we were told an absolute pack of lies about outside.'

'I wonder,' Chris mused.

'What?'

'I wonder if there's any way of going back; of getting people out?'

'Doubt it mate,' Jay said sadly. 'You heard Anilla. Anyway, would you know the way, even if we could get out of Portum?'

'You think we're trapped here?' Chris asked.

'In a way,' Jay nodded. 'I mean, not many folk leave, do they?'

'So we've swapped one prison for another?'

'Sometimes I think so,' Jay sighed. 'I'd love to be able to come and go as we please, wouldn't you?'

'I would, but I suppose the wild dragons are dangerous, that's probably why they keep us here. I know Anilla and some of the others go on trips looking for plants and stuff, that's how they found me and Bertram you know, saved us from being attacked by some big feline.'

'I heard the tales,' Jay said. 'You were quite the news you know, when you got here. Farle and Ishy were full of how you took a swing at Jax,' he chuckled. 'And Jax was so upset, it was his expedition you see, and I think he was hoping to get some recognition for it.'

'It feels like that was a long time ago,' Chris said. 'But it's only been a few weeks, not even two months really.' He shook his head, thinking how much his life had changed in such a short time.

Chapter 10 – The Gathering

Over the next couple of weeks, Chris and Jay worked harder than ever. Garad assessed the sheets of paper they'd made, over half were put back into the mulch bin. Then they began learning how to trim and sew the remaining pages into sections, ready to be made into books.

'I swear I've made more holes in the ends of my fingers than I have in the paper,' Chris said one night as they were walking home.

Jay rubbed his fingertips gently. 'I know what you mean,' he said, 'I think we need some of those hard leather finger protector things that Garad and Edwin use.'

Chris pointed at a string of flags, fluttering in the light breeze. 'What's going on? Anilla didn't say there was anything happening tonight, did she?'

'Nope,' Jay shook his head, 'let's hurry up and get ready, then we can go and be nosey.' He broke into a trot.

'Hey! Wait for me!' Chris galloped to catch up.

They got home and were washed, changed and on their way for their evening meal in record time. As they entered the main dining area they saw people placing lanterns and putting up more strings of flags. The Council Hall was festooned with brightly coloured banners and there was a low level of excited chattering.

Chris saw Anilla making her way over to them and waved at her in greeting.

'Here she comes,' Jay said, 'she's bound to know what's going on. Can we get food though? I'm starving!'

He turned away before Chris could answer and was in the queue before Anilla made it to join them.

'Hi,' Chris said, giving her a big smile. 'How are you? Had a good day? What's going on here?' He waved an arm at the flags.

'Hello Chris,' she smiled at Jay, who waved a serving spoon at her by way of greeting. 'We're getting ready for the big autumn Gathering,' she told him.

'What's that?' he asked, handing her a plate as the line moved along.

'Well, it's a big, you know, gathering,' Anilla teased, spooning potatoes onto her plate.

Beside her, Chris groaned, 'It's going to be one of those nights, is it? Can't you just tell me?'

'I will, I promise, let's get sat down first though, ok?'

Chris nodded and began loading his own plate with vegetables and slices of roasted meats. Picking up a mug of hot Harbatu last, he made his way to the table Jay had chosen. Anilla was already taking her place. Once he was seated, he looked expectantly at her.

'Oh alright,' she said with a sigh, 'can't a girl eat her dinner first?'

'Nope,' Jay said, loading his fork and beginning on his own meal.

'Well, a gathering is when people from other settlements nearby come and join us. There's a chance for crafters to meet, traders come too, so if there's anything you need...' Her voice trailed off for a moment before she continued. 'Then there's an evening of songs, tellings and so on,' she said, 'but, with this being the end of summer, this one is a bigger gathering than usual. We'll have more people coming in, there'll be entertainers too. Last time we had fire eaters!' She said, her eyes sparkling.

Chris and Jay hadn't thought about other settlements, much less the people who lived in them travelling to Portum.

'I've only just got used to how many people are in Portum,' Chris said, 'how many more are there likely to be?'

'Oh our numbers can double or triple,' Anilla said cheerfully, 'folk'll start arriving tomorrow probably, and the Gathering proper is on Saturday, all day and into the night and Sunday too. They'll all start leaving after lunch time on Sunday, depending on the river levels, then back to normal on Monday. It's a big weekend.'

'What happens then, at the Gathering?' Jay asked.

'Well, there's tellings, as we have here anyway, but tellers will come in with new stories. Then there's the feast of course, and dancing, and entertainments. We put out a big floor for the dancing, it's made of wooden planks, makes a lovely noise when you do the sets.'

'Sets?' Chris and Jay both looked blankly at her.

'Dances have set sequences of steps,' she explained, 'well, some of them do, and they have stamping, or tapping, and then the men lift the ladies and the sound when we all land together, it's amazing,' Anilla was smiling happily.

'Are these Gathers where people find mates?' Jay asked her.

'Sometimes,' she nodded.

'How about you?' Chris asked, 'have you met some-one at a Gathering?'

'I did once,' she admitted, 'but it didn't come to anything. He didn't want to leave his home, and there's no way I would ever leave Portum. So...' she shrugged.

'So,' Jay said, 'this is Thursday, people will start arriving tomorrow and there'll be trading caravans?'

'What are they?' Chris wanted to know.

'They're travelling tradesmen, they go to all the gatherings and sell their wares.'

Chris felt his mind start spinning, he had so many questions.

'How do we get things from these traders?' Jay asked between mouthfuls.

'You barter,' Anilla said, 'or use coins, if you have any.'

'That's us done then,' Jay said to Chris, 'we have nothing to barter with, and I don't have coins, do you?' Chris shook his head.

'I'm sure Garad and Edwin won't let you be stuck,' Anilla said, so merrily that the boys looked at her with suspicion. She merely smiled and continued eating her dinner.

'Where do the traders come from?' Chris asked. 'Do they live in one of the other settlements?'

'No,' Anilla shook her head, 'they don't have permanent homes, they go from one settlement to the next.'

'How do they find out about the gatherings then?'

Jay asked.

'Gatherings normally happen on a fairly set schedule, so, unless we have really bad weather, or lots of attacks, they will go ahead and the traders know it.' She told him. 'They have regular camps in safe places and they do good business while they're here. They think the risk is worth it.'

'And all these people are coming to Portum for just one day?' Chris shook his head, 'I don't get it, isn't it a long way to come, and isn't it dangerous for them?'

'It can be,' Anilla said, 'but everyone likes getting together. Crafters swap ideas and news of their crafts. New masters are made and journeymen are given new assignments, as we're all together. And it's an opportunity for the general council to meet and discuss any issues. It might seem a long journey for a short time, but it's worth it and, to be honest, it's rarely just the one night.'

Chris and Jay let all this sink in as they sipped their cooling batu. They sat for a long while after they'd eaten, watching the preparations for the Gathering. Long tables were being set up at one side of the dining area, which Anilla said was for the use of the brewers.

'There'll be lots of barrels hauled across from the brewers hall,' she told them. 'Always popular. Then all these tables will be put to the side so there's a clear space in the middle, which is where the floor gets put down.'

Chris felt a glimmer of excitement begin in his stomach. His very first Gathering.

***

Friday morning arrived and Jay and Chris wandered towards their breakfast. Work crews were already busy, a huge pile of wooden boards was stacked at the edge of the dining area and tables were being lifted out of the way as soon as diners had cleared them. The boys ate quickly, standing with their batu to watch the base for the dancing floor being laid.

After breakfast, as they walked towards the river, they saw temporary shelters being built. They were canvas constructions which reminded Chris of the tent in the dining area. Some of the new tents were square, some triangular, all had brightly coloured flags fluttering from the top.

'Mornin', you two's in good time today,' Garad said as they walked in, 'seen the tents have ye?'

'Yes, we saw them. Are they for the visitors?' Chris asked.

'Yup,' Edwin was grinning, 'it's gonna be a bit lively this weekend lads.'

'We're really looking forward to it,' Jay said, 'our first Gathering.'

Edwin and Garad shared a look. Edwin gave the barest nod to Garad before sauntering off to look at the book he'd been working on the previous day.

'Now lads,' Garad said gruffly, 'you know there's going to be traders and whatnot this weekend?'

They nodded.

'Well, er,' he paused, 'you must have noticed that yeh've not been paid so far.'

'Paid?' Jay looked confused.

'Why would we be paid?' Chris asked.

'Oh my, weren't wages mentioned at all?' Garad said, sitting down heavily on his stool.

Chris and Jay shook their heads. 'No one's mentioned money to me at all,' Chris said.

'Well lads, I know in the caves currency was rare and you were expected to work just for your bed and board, so to speak.' He looked at the boys, who both nodded. It was true, they had never been paid, no one had. They were given food, somewhere to live, and looked after, and this was considered to be enough.

'There was no money,' Chris said. 'You know what Salutem's like. But then, there was nothing we needed money for. The idea was taught to us as an ancient practice.'

'I know lad, but here, things are different.' Garad paused to let this begin to sink in. 'Here, you gets paid for your work, the amount you get depends on where you're working and how good you are, how advanced in your craft you are.'

Chris and Jay nodded, glancing at each other. This was getting interesting.

'Well,' Garad went on, 'as you work for me, and paper crafting is seen as an important occupation,'

'We're important!' Edwin interrupted. 'We are what is known in these parts as elite, that means that er...'

'We're important,' Garad finished for him. 'It also means we gets paid well for what we do.'

Chris felt his mind whirling. Jay looked stunned.

'Money was just for the high ups in Barlang,' Jay said, 'we saw some coins once but they were historical artefacts.'

'Well, these ain't no artefacts,' Garad said, hefting a leather pouch in his hand. They could hear a metallic jingle from within. Garad emptied the contents of the pouch onto his table. Bronze and silver coins clattered into a heap, among them a couple of gold coins glinted. Some were round, some were many sided, and some had holes in the middle.

'Wow,' Chris breathed, gazing at them.

Garad began picking up the coins and showing them to the boys. 'These small bronze ones, they're pennies,' he said, handing them an example each. 'These silver ones are worth ten of the pennies and are called shillings.' Again, he handed each of the boys a coin.

Chris turned the coins over in his hand, feeling the weight, examining the designs and admiring the shine. 'Do the smiths make these?' he asked softly.

'Aye, they do, well some of 'em,' Edwin said, 'they have to prove themselves before they're allowed near currency, else there could be problems.'

Chris nodded. He was thinking of Bertram, who hadn't mentioned this as an occupational choice when he'd been talking to them about the smith craft.

The many-sided pale golden coins with a hole in the middle were called tanners and were worth fifteen pennies, and the gold coins were pounds and worth a hundred pennies. They were surprisingly heavy when Chris handled them. He gave all the coins back to Garad.

'Why are they called tanners?' Jay asked.

'Cos the tanners usually ask that amount for their wares,' Edwin said. 'Over time the name stuck.'

Chris and Jay nodded, they were watching Garad, who had produced two more pouches, one clearly marked with a 'J', the other bore a 'C', these pouches were empty. He began counting out coins into each. 'There you go,' he handed one to Jay before popping a couple of extra coins into the second pouch and handing it to Chris. 'You gets more cos you've been with us a bit longer,' he said with a smile. He quickly made two piles of the remaining coins, putting the larger pile into his own pouch and handing the rest of the coins over to Edwin.

'Thank you,' Chris said, weighing the pouch in his hand.

'Do we get paid every time there's a Gathering?' Jay asked.

'You get paid every week usually,' Edwin said, 'but we've been holding off with you, knowing this was coming up. But you're good lads, and you've worked hard. You deserve to enjoy your weekend.'

Garad nodded, 'Aye, you've not done badly, for young uns,' he said. As he rarely handed out praise, Chris and Jay beamed.

'This is brilliant!' Jay said, 'thank you.'

'Now, hand 'em back,' Garad said, holding out his hand for the pouches, 'I'll put them in my drawer for the day and you can have 'em as we leave tonight. Ok?'

Reluctantly, they both handed back their pouches and went to put on their heavy cotton aprons.

The day dragged and Chris found it difficult to focus on what he was doing. When he stabbed himself for the tenth time that morning he swore quietly, gently rubbing his sore finger tips.

'P'raps you could get yourself some o' these at the Gathering,' Edwin waggled his fingers at him, the tips were covered in hard leather caps, Edwin called them thimbles.

'I'll have to see if I can find some,' Chris nodded, 'cos this is really painful.'

'Tanners should have 'em,' Garad said, 'if not, you can ask to have some made, but that's more expensive o'course.'

'They'd make them just for us?' Jay asked, 'I mean, are there other crafts who use them?'

'Oh aye,' Garad said, 'weavers, some of the smiths, anyone who does any sort of sewing, even some of the fishers use 'em when they're mending nets and...whatever it is they does over there.' He grinned at Jay, 'you'd know more than me on that score young Jay.'

Jay laughed, 'I can't say I saw anyone using those in my time with the fishers,' he said, 'mind you, I wasn't really looking, I was on other duties. You know, the smelly jobs.'

'They're all smelly jobs over there, ain't they?' Edwin asked.

Chris had never heard so much chatter in the usually quiet paper hall. It was an hour earlier than usual when Garad went to his desk and removed the pouches of coins.

'Here,' he said, lobbing them to the boys, 'I reckon it's knocking off time. Got to go get ready for tonight.'

'I thought the Gathering was tomorrow?' Jay said.

'Aye, officially, but there's likely to be lots of extra folks around this evening, and I don't doubt there'll be dancing and suchlike.'

Chris and Jay didn't take telling twice, they tidied their work tables, removing their aprons and hanging them on the hooks behind them. Then the four of them left together, Garad made sure the windows were barred and the door locked.

'Can't be too careful,' he said, seeing their questioning looks, 'Portum folk wouldn't bother us at all, they know better, but visitors sometimes think it's a good idea to nose around in our craft halls and things have been known to go missing. So now...' he patted his pocket where the key lay. 'Off we go then.'

They walked together back towards Portum village. Chris could see laden boats pulled ashore and as they watched a strange dragon arrived and landed near the river. Several people clambered down from its back and began untying bundles. Then it leapt skywards, wings churning the air as it fought for height.

'I thought Portum was difficult to get into,' Jay said, 'I was surprised to find this is where the big Gatherings take place.'

'Tis difficult,' Edwin nodded, 'unless you've got a boat or a dragon, and most of the other settlements have both, so.' He shrugged and looked across to the sea of tents on the other side of the river. 'Filling up nicely,' he said, 'traders should start arriving afore long.' As he spoke more boats rounded the bend in the river and they could hear the shouts of Portum folk greeting the newcomers.

'This is us,' Chris said as they reached their cottage, 'we'll maybe see you this evening?'

Garad and Edwin nodded, 'oh, we'll be there lad, can't beat a few beers and the chance of a good chinwag with other crafters.'

They said their goodbyes and the boys went into their house to make ready for the evening. They had hardly closed the door when there was a knock and they heard Anilla's voice.

Chris rushed to open the door and she almost ran inside.

'Are you ok?' Chris asked in alarm.

'I yes....no....not really....I don't know,' Anilla looked as if she were about to burst into tears.

'Come and sit down,' Jay said, 'what's going on?'

'I'm fine, honestly,' Anilla insisted, perching on the edge of the couch, 'but..'

'But?' Chris prompted.

Anilla sighed. 'You remember me telling you the other day about the boy I met at a Gather? The one who wouldn't leave his home to be with me?'

'Yes,' they both nodded.

'Well he's here. I just saw him talking to Narilka, but he didn't see me. I could hear him though, asking about me, about my training.' One hand plucked at the nearest cushion.

'That's good though, isn't it?'

Anilla shook her head, 'I don't want to see him, I don't want anything to do with him,' she said. 'I wasn't important enough before, and if I'm being honest, neither was he.' She paused and took a deep breath. 'But it seems word has got out that I'm being given extra training by Fallaren and Narilka. Perhaps he thinks they want me to be the next leader, I don't know but suddenly he thinks I'm more of a catch.'

'No!' Chris said, more loudly than he'd intended, 'if he wants to be with you, then he should want you, not some position you may or may not hold at some point in the future.' He felt himself growing hot. Jay and Anilla looked at him in surprise. 'I only mean,' he said, drawing a long, deep breath, 'that you're a really lovely person Anilla, you've been so kind and friendly to me since I got here, I don't know how I'd have managed without you. I'd hate to see you stuck with someone whose only interest in you was your future position.'

'Thank you,' Anilla said, her cheeks flushing pink, 'I like you too, both of you,' she added hurriedly.

'Yeah, yeah, I get it,' Jay said, 'Chris is your boy wonder, and I'm just the tag along. I know.' He shook his head in mock sadness, glancing up at her out of the corner of his eyes.

The ghost of a smile played on Anilla's lips.

'What are you going to do?' Chris asked, 'It's a Gathering, you can't hide away all weekend,'

'I don't know,' she said, a frown creasing her forehead.

'Are you sure you want nothing to do with him?' Chris asked.

'Yes.'

'Then why not have a word with Fallaren or Narilka, maybe they could put him off a bit?'

'Why would they do that?'

'Well, if you make it clear you have no interest in him and he keeps hanging around being a nuisance, I just thought maybe they could tell him to clear off or something?'

'I don't know,' she said sadly.

'Look, if he starts bugging you, just find us, we'll look after you,' Jay said brightly.

'Might be more of a case of you looking after us,' Chris laughed, 'we've never experienced a Gathering before, we might get lost or something.'

'Lost? How can you get lost?' Anilla was smiling now, 'it's still Portum, just with more people and things to do.'

'We've seen the tents,' Jay said, 'looks like it's going to be busy.'

'Oh, the tents are just the half of it,' Anilla said. 'A lot of the visitors will bring their own shelters with them, but we put some out too. It's like a mini village over there. I think it's pretty, with all the flags fluttering. The dragons don't like it though, it takes their Portum space and the wilds can be attracted by the extra noise and activity. We have to put on extra patrols during a Gathering.'

'Will riders be there?' Chris asked, hoping he might see them, and possibly even a dragon.

'Yes, more than likely. You won't be seeing dragons

though, if that's what you're hoping. Too many folk around, makes accidents more likely.'

'Fair,' Jay said, nodding, 'now, we'd better get ourselves washed and changed. You gonna wait here for us?' he asked Anilla, who nodded.

'If you don't mind,' she said, 'I won't be in the way, will I?'

'Course you won't,' Chris said, 'we won't be long.'

Both boys vanished into their rooms and soon Jay could be heard singing in the bathing room. Chris stuck his head out of his bedroom door. 'His singing hasn't improved, has it?'

She shook her head, giving him a tired little smile and he disappeared back into his room. Anilla wandered around before sitting in one of the chairs, arranging the cushions to her liking. Sighing, she gazed idly out of the window.

It wasn't long before the three friends were wandering together along the street towards the dining area. The nearer they got to the main area, the busier it became. All the tables around the cleared floor area were full, mostly they saw strangers sitting there.

'I see an empty table,' Jay said, 'you two grab some batu, I'll get seats.' He darted away, leaving Anilla and Chris to queue for drinks. To save time they picked up a big jug of batu and three cups and made their way over to Jay, who was looking rather pleased with himself. 'I got a good one!' he said as they joined him, 'think we can hang onto it all night?'

'You probably won't want to,' Anilla said, 'not once

the traders get set up, and our own crafters set their stalls out. I know the Gathering proper is tomorrow, but some will want to get started early.'

Chris poured them all a drink and they sat quietly for a moment, looking around at all the strangers. 'I didn't know there were this many people in the world,' he said, eyeing a strangely dressed group wandering past them. Their dark clothing and long, black cloaks seemed out of place in Portum, with its fluttering flags and cheerful, colourfully dressed people. Chris noted the large brooches which held their cloaks at the neck. Dark stones glittered in the late afternoon sun, Chris thought they looked a bit menacing. 'Who are they?' he asked, indicating the group with a nod of his head.

'They're the council leaders, from Escal.' Anilla told him. 'That's a settlement on the other side of the mountains. Must be important business to attend to, it's a long journey.'

'Council?' Jay queried.

'Yeah, you mentioned this Council before, what is it?' Chris asked.

'All the leaders of the settlements are on the council; they make the rules every settlement observes. These folk are in charge overall. They take themselves very seriously.' She watched the group quietly. 'I do hope there's not going to be trouble,' she said.

Chris and Jay watched the dark procession too, then Chris shook himself. 'There are so many people,' he said, 'it's getting more crowded than Salutem ever felt!'

'It's going to be busier than this,' Anilla said, 'you sure you're going to be ok?'

'I think so,' Chris said, 'I mean, I'm used to crowds I guess, it's just the not knowing people. I've only just started to know folk around Portum, now there's more strangers!'

'You won't speak to most of them,' Anilla said, 'they're here in their family or craft groups and they tend to stick to them, unless they're looking for a partner of course.' She was looking fixedly at a group on the far side of the dancing square. Chris followed her gaze.

'Is that him?' he asked quietly.

Anilla nodded. 'The tall one with dark hair and the strange little beard,' she said. 'I don't know what I saw in him, I really don't.'

Chris saw the young man turn to look straight at Anilla. Pretending that he hadn't seen him, Chris casually slipped an arm around her shoulders and pulled her towards him. 'Just play along,' he whispered as she stiffened at such familiarity. She looked up at him, saw him wink, and laughed, leaning against his shoulder. Chris saw a sour look on the other man's face, then he turned away. 'While he's here, let's stick close together,' he said, giving her shoulders a brief squeeze before releasing her.

Anilla sat up straight and nodded. 'Alright. Thank you.'

Then they both turned their attention to Jay, who had almost choked on his batu.

'What was all that about?' he demanded once he'd stopped coughing.

'Just making a point to that lad,' Chris said, nodding in the direction of where he'd seen the young man in question. 'If Anilla wants nothing to do with him, let him think she's moved on with someone else.' He gave a cheeky grin as Jay shook his head, laughing.

***

The evening drew on. Delicious smells began wafting towards them, and Jay's stomach rumbled loudly. He wandered off to get food, leaving Chris and Anilla at the table.

Chris watched Anilla nervously scanning the crowds. 'Are you ok?' he asked.

'What? Oh, yes,' Anilla said, though her voice wobbled slightly.

'You're worried about him?' Chris asked.

Anilla barely nodded. 'What do I say to him if he tries talking to me?' she said, her voice was so quiet Chris had to lean in to hear her.

'You tell him to go away,' he said robustly, 'you tell him you're too good for him and that you want nothing to do with him.'

'Too good for him?' Anilla gave a half laugh which caught in her throat.

'Yes.' Chris nodded firmly. 'You're worth more than some lad who can't leave his parents for you.'

Anilla looked surprised but said nothing. Instead she paid close attention to the empty cup in front of her.

Jay returned with a laden plate. 'Go get yours,' he urged, 'before the hoards descend and there's none left. Hey, are you alright?' He said, noticing Anilla's sad face.

'Yes, I'm fine thank you. There's always plenty of

food,' Anilla said, but she and Chris rose and went to get their dinners.

'Look who it is,' said a nasal voice behind them in the queue.

Chris felt Anilla stiffen beside him, then she turned. 'Hello Jorash,' she said coolly, 'I wasn't expecting to see you in Portum again.'

'Wasn't expecting to be here,' he said, 'but I thought I'd look you up, see how you're doing.'

'I'm just fine, thank you for asking.' Her voice wobbled a little and she took a breath. 'I'm sure you could have sent a message, if that's what you wanted to know, rather than trekking all this way.' She turned her back on Jorash and linked her arm through Chris.

Behind them, Chris heard Jorash sniff. 'I was hoping,' he began, but was interrupted by the squeal of a violin.

Chris winced. 'What was that? Sounds like someone's in pain.'

'They're getting ready to play music for the dancing,' Anilla said, 'I believe it's called tuning up.'

'They need to hurry up then,' Chris said, rubbing his ear.

He could hear Jorash tutting and sighing, then he tried again. 'Anilla, as I was saying, I was hoping...'

Anilla spun round to face him. 'Well don't!' She spat the words out. 'I didn't matter to you before. Nothing has changed. I know now that you didn't matter to me either. Now, excuse us please. I do hope you enjoy the Gather.' She turned back to Chris and leant against him;

he could feel her trembling.

'Are you ok honey?' he asked in a concerned tone, just loud enough for Jorash to hear.

'Yes, yes I'm fine,' she responded, 'come on, it's our turn now, let's get our dinners and go sit down.'

Back at the table, Jay was all excited questions. 'Was that him? What did he want? Anilla, you looked like a wild feline, I could see the sparks! Are you both alright?'

Anilla filled him in while Chris began eating.

'The nerve!' Jay said indignantly. 'Well, you can do so much better for yourself than that long streak of nothing!'

Anilla smiled, 'Actually, as far as he's concerned, I already have,' she said. 'Haven't I honey?' She nudged Chris.

Chris felt his cheeks growing hot but he grinned. 'It seemed to work,' he said.

They applied themselves to their meals and silence fell over the little group.

***

As the evening wore on, more people arrived and Portum became crowded and noisier than Salutem had ever been. Chris sat watching the ebb and flow. Crafters were greeting each other, old friends hugging, and the level of noise grew steadily. The brewers heaved barrels onto their tables and began serving. Brewers from other villages joined them and good-natured competition was evident as they tasted each other's wares.

A group of musicians took to the stage and began

playing a lively tune. Chris was very pleased they'd got the tune after the terrible screeching he'd heard earlier. Shortly the dance floor was full of couples, some were accomplished dancers, others obviously struggling to remember the steps.

After a while sitting and watching, Anilla suggested they take a walk and see what was going on. The three of them vacated their table, which was immediately taken by a noisy group.

As they walked away from the dancing, they could see rows of tables set out, each with its own bright fabric roof. Some stalls held trader's wares and the three took their time wandering up and down, inspecting the goods for sale.

'There'll be lots more traders tomorrow,' Anilla told them as they walked past several empty tables before darting away in the direction of a stall laden with bolts of fabric.

'Jay, look!' Chris nudged his friend, 'there's some of those finger end protectors Garad and Edwin were talking about.' They approached the stall and picked up the protectors. The leather felt smooth under their fingertips, but not hardened as much as Garad's had been. The trader watched them carefully, eager for a sale, but they shook their heads at him and moved away.

'No good?' Anilla asked, her hands full with a package of fabric.

'Nah, too soft, they wouldn't last five minutes.' Jay said, 'we'll find some, or we'll find our own tanners and ask to have some made. That's what Garad suggested.'

'Worth a look though,' Chris said, eyeing Anilla's

package, 'what have you been buying?'

'Fabric for a new dress,' she showed them a corner, 'thought it might be nice to have something pretty to wear at these events, rather than,' she waved a hand at herself, indicating her wrap skirt and simple top.

'You look alright though,' Jay said casually.

'Thanks, I think,' Anilla laughed.

Smells assailed their noses. Somewhere, onions were being fried.

'Food!' Jay set off at a trot.

'That boy is always hungry,' Chris laughed as he watched his friend vanish into the crowds.

'You've got a decent appetite yourself,' Anilla said. 'You've still not caught up from the starvation rations they had you on in those caves.'

Jay arrived back and handed them both a long sausage in a boat shaped bread roll. The sausage was adorned with piles of the fried onions and some red sauce. Chris sniffed it suspiciously.

'It's a fruity sauce,' Anilla told him. 'Goes well with the sausage, try it.' She took a bite of her own, sighing as half her onions fell to the floor.

'This is good,' Jay mumbled, his mouth full of bread and sausage.

Chris took a careful bite and chewed slowly. 'It's alright I suppose,' he said, wrinkling his nose slightly. 'I like the onions, but you can have mine if you like Jay.' He held it out to his friend, who took it from him eagerly and began munching.

194

'Hey! Chris!' The shout was loud enough to be heard above the noise of the people on the stalls calling their wares. He looked around, seeing the familiar face approaching through the crowd.

'Hi Bertram,' he said as soon as they were close enough. 'You ok? What do you make of all this?'

'It's great, isn't it!' Bertram said, then saw Jay eating. 'What's that?' Anilla explained and he shot off to the stall and was back in moments clutching his own. 'This is good!' he said around a mouthful of sausage and onions.

'Chris wasn't so keen, were you?' Anilla said, 'gave his away.'

Jay looked hopefully at Bertram, who shook his head. 'No chance matey, get your own.'

'He's already had two!' Chris protested, but Jay was already walking back to the stall for another. 'He'll burst!'

'Having a good time?' Bertram asked.

Chris shrugged. 'Not bad, be better tomorrow I reckon, when everyone gets here. Be busy mind.'

Bertram nodded, swallowing the last of his snack. 'The smith lads were saying it gets busy, we're having our own stall you know, well, some of the others are, I've not been here long enough yet, but I'll be stopping by, see what's what. You never know, could be me next time.'

'Yeah,' Chris said, surprised by Bertram's enthusiasm. 'We don't have a stall this time, but Jay and I have only been with them for a short while, by the next Gather our production should be up enough for us to have a stall perhaps.' He frowned, he'd not really thought about it before, but would anyone here be able to afford their books or paper? Were they allowed to sell it? He made a note to talk to Garad and Edwin about the possibilities of selling at the next Gathering.

Bertram joined their group as they slowly made their way back towards the dining area and the music. Voices were raised in song and, as they were looking round for seats, Chris saw Narilka waving to them. He waved back and she beckoned them to join her. He nudged Anilla, 'Narilka wants us to go over to her,' he shouted in her ear. Normal conversation was impossible.

Anilla nodded and, after catching Jay and Bertram's attention, the four made their way around the dance floor and over to Narilka, who was seated with Fallaren and the Council leaders they'd seen earlier beneath a canvas roof.

'We have seats!' Narilka announced, her voice slurred slightly, 'come, sit with me and tell me how you like your first Gathering.'

Chris and Jay shared a glance, but before they could start speaking, Bertram jumped in.

'It's fantastic!' he said enthusiastically, 'I love meeting all these new people, and seeing the stalls and trying the foods.' His voice had taken on a manic edge.

'I like it too,' Chris said guardedly, noting the glances they were getting from the serious leaders, 'but it's very busy and I'm not sure about being with so many strangers.'

Narilka nodded, 'I understand Chris,' she said, 'I was like that at first too.' She appeared to be having trouble sitting up straight and was leaning against the table with her elbow.

Bertram looked a little deflated, Chris wondered why. 'Are you ok?' he mouthed at Bertram, who nodded curtly. He pulled a stool from beneath the table and sat a little way from Narilka, apparently intent on the dancing.

'Come, sit with me,' Narilka patted the seat next to her and pulled at Chris' arm. Bemused, he sat down and smiled a little nervously at her. 'How are you liking it here?' she asked him, leaning towards him. Her was breath sharp with wine.

'I like it,' he said, leaning back a little, trying not to let his nose wrinkle, 'I'm really enjoying my work, and the people are lovely here. And I like the sunshine,' he added, 'now I've got used to it.' He gave a short laugh and Jay joined in.

Bertram shifted his stool closer to Chris and lay his arm heavily across his shoulders. 'It's good here, isn't it bro?' He said. 'I'm glad we got away, got out. Much better in Portum.'

Chris nodded and shot a surprised look at Jay, who grinned and shrugged.

Anilla, who had disappeared for a minute, re-appeared and took a seat on the other side of Narilka. She placed a mug of batu in front of her, and a jug of water with a cup. 'I thought you might appreciate this,' she said quietly to the leader, who smiled her thanks and picked up the batu, taking a sip.

'Head'll be sore in the morning,' Narilka said, 'but it's the first real Gathering in a while. Too many storms and attacks you know.'

Anilla nodded understandingly and they settled themselves to watch the dancing, even attempting to join in with the singing, although Bertram, Jay and Chris had no idea of the words to most of the songs. The moon was high in the sky before the players stopped and people began drifting away to their beds.

Fallaren helped a protesting Narilka to her feet, and they walked slowly towards their quarters above the council chambers.

'Where are you sleeping tonight?' Chris asked Bertram. 'You're not walking right the way over to the smith hall are you? It'll be breakfast time before you get to bed.'

'I dunno,' Bertram said, 'I hadn't thought about it. I could stay in that place we were in at the start I guess.' He looked questioningly at Anilla.

'Sorry,' she said with a shake of her head, 'we have new folk in there now.'

'Ah.' Bertram sagged. 'What should I do?'

'You could always stay with us,' Chris offered. 'We have a new place now, with a nice comfy couch, and it's all yours if you'd like it.'

'That'd be great,' Bertram said, 'you sure that's ok?' He looked at Jay, who nodded his assent.

The four made their way towards Anilla's home first.

'Did you like your first gathering evening?' Anilla asked them.

'Yeah, it was alright,' Jay said, 'Narilka was a bit the worse for wear, wasn't she?'

'She was a little drunk tonight.' Anilla admitted.

'She was funny,' Chris said, 'suddenly I was her

favourite person! I don't think I've ever been anyone's favourite person before.' He gave a laugh which turned into a yawn. 'What did Narilka mean that this is the first real Gathering for a while? I thought you said they were on a regular schedule?' he asked.

'The last couple had to be cancelled,' Anilla told him. 'We had bad weather, and trouble with the wilds, a lot of attacks. The council decided it was unsafe to travel and gather in big numbers. So we didn't.'

'Are the wilds still attacking a lot?' Chris asked, remembering the attack he'd witnessed just after he arrived in Portum.

'It's not as bad as it was,' she said. 'Don't know what got into them. We really do need to find a way to get them under control. Some folks want them exterminated,' she continued sadly, 'but really we need to find a way to make them leave us alone. Our dragons and riders are a great deterrent though.'

'Shame we have to sit here, waiting for them to attack,' Chris said thoughtfully. 'We're like sitting targets. Couldn't our dragons go and find the wilds and do something to stop them before they start?'

'It has been talked about, but so far no one's done anything.' Anilla told him. 'It would possibly be a suicide mission and we don't want to risk lives unnecessarily.'

Chris nodded thoughtfully.

The boys dropped Anilla off, seeing her safely into her house before they set off to their own cottage.

Jay flung open the door and ushered Bertram inside. 'Here we are Bertie, home sweet home.'

Chris winced at Jay's use of the nickname but Bertram seemed unfazed. He was looking around as Chris and Jay lit a couple of lamps.

'This isn't half bad, is it?' Bertram said, throwing himself onto the couch and making himself comfortable.

'We like it Bertram,' Chris said, sitting at the opposite end of the couch and looking pointedly at Jay. 'It's certainly more comfortable than the first place.'

'Comfier than anything in Salutem too,' Bertram said. He took a deep breath before continuing. 'Look, Chris, everyone here calls me Bert or Bertie, except you of course, but I quite like it.'

Chris' eyes widened. 'You'd never let anyone shorten your name back home,' he said.

'Father wouldn't let anyone shorten my name,' Bertram corrected, 'but I like it. It's like marking the new start I've made here, so you don't need to worry when folk call me Bertie,' he grinned at Jay.

'Ok then, if that's what you prefer Bertram.' Chris shook his head. 'Might take me a while bro.'

Bert grinned. 'Take your time bro, took me a while to get used to it too. Now, where do you two sleep? Cos at the moment you're sitting on my bed!'

Jay and Chris turned out the lamps, said good night and went to bed. Before long the house was silent except for gentle snores coming from the couch.

Chapter 11 - An
unscheduled visit

The next morning dawned bright and fair; a brisk breeze making the flags dance merrily. Portum was eerily quiet as Jay and Chris made their way towards their breakfast.

'Where is everyone?' Chris asked.

'Probably sleeping off the beer from last night,' Jay said.

Chris nodded; he had seen evidence of heavy beer consumption the previous evening. The various brewers and vintners had plenty of empty barrels to show for the first night of the Gather. There would be many sore heads this morning.

The smells of breakfast wafted to them and they hurried their pace.

'I'm starving,' Jay announced as they picked up plates and began serving themselves.

'You're always hungry,' Chris said, 'although how you can be after eating a huge dinner last night and, what was it, three sausage and onion things?'

'Made me more peckish than ever this morning,' Jay grinned as he spooned scrambled eggs onto his plate and topped them with several slices of bacon and a hunk of bread.

Chris shook his head, loading his own plate with his usual breakfast, although he did slip an extra sausage onto his plate. 'I wonder when our appetites will level off,' he said, picking up a mug of batu, 'It's been weeks and I'm still eating like a dragon.'

'Dunno,' Jay shrugged, 'luckily, they don't mind here. Imagine doing this back in the caves?' He munched on a sausage as they made their way to the nearest table.

As they ate, they could see more boats coming up the river, each with coloured flags flying from the helm.

'More traders by the look of it,' Jay said, 'the different colours of the flags tell you where they're from and what they do. I haven't got it worked out yet, but Anilla knows. I think yellow means weavers, but I'm not sure.'

Chris sat back and looked more intently at the newcomers, who were pulling their boats onto the gravel banks. 'I never knew there could be so many people,' he said quietly, 'back in Salutem the population is controlled, but there always seemed to be lots of folk about. Here, there just seems to be more and more.' He shook his head, watching in fascination as the latest boat was unloaded.

'Was the same in Barlang. What do you want to do this morning?' Jay asked.

'I've no idea,' Chris laughed, 'never had free time before. What do you want to do?'

'Keep out of the way for a while,' Jay said, 'it's going to be a long day I reckon, but it'll take them a while to get sorted. Fancy having a walk this morning? We could get away from all the folk, possibly go have a look at the dragons?' he looked hopefully at Chris.

'Oh I don't know about that.' Chris said warily. 'Fallaren told Anilla off for taking me to see the eggs without telling him or Narilka first.'

'We don't have to go see the eggs, just the dragons.

Oh go on, it'll be fun, better than hanging around here all day and getting roped in to goodness knows what.'

Chris chewed his breakfast in silence, frowning thoughtfully.

'Oh come on Chris,' Jay urged, 'we can be there and back before anyone misses us, and it'll be good to stretch our legs. Come on, what do you say?'

Chris nodded reluctantly. 'Alright,' he said, 'I'd love to get another look at them. Haven't been anywhere near since that first day when Anilla took me.'

They finished their breakfasts and left, calling cheery greetings to the few they saw heading blearily towards the dining area. They received grunts in return and laughed as they ran round the corner of the last house and headed out of Portum village towards the farmlands and the cliffs which housed the dragons.

They walked past fields of crops, neither of them knew what they were. In one field a farmer was walking behind two huge horses which were pulling a machine. Behind them the crops lay in neat rows on the ground. A couple of men with long forks followed them, expertly picking up the fallen crops and tossing them onto a large, flat wooden platform which was being drawn along by a tired looking horse. Chris and Jay leant on the fence and watched for a while.

'Fascinating, isn't it,' Jay said at last.

'Hypnotic,' Chris agreed, 'but the sun's getting warm now, and the back of my neck's feeling it. Let's get going, shall we?'

They passed fields of cattle, and Jay attempted to

name the different types.

'These are cows,' he said, indicating a group of large animals with brown and cream splotches. There were youngsters among the adults, cavorting in the sun. Jay assured Chris that these were puppies.

'Are you sure?' Chris asked doubtfully.

'Yes. Well, I think so,' Jay grinned and shrugged.

The next field held, 'Pigs!' Jay announced confidently. 'I remember these guys, cos they don't half pong!' He waved a hand beneath his nose.

Chris watched the pigs, fascinated by the way their back ends wiggled as they walked. 'I reckon,' he said slowly, 'that if I hadn't started with Garad and Edwin, I might have enjoyed looking after the animals here.'

Jay looked at him in disbelief. 'This lot stink worse than anything I did with the fishers,' he said.

'Bet you wouldn't notice it after a while though.' Chris countered.

'Maybe not, but everyone else would!' Jay held his nose delicately and they both laughed.

A large pig stood up and around her a large group of her young ran, squealing and falling over one another.

'And those are?' Chris looked expectantly at Jay.

'Piglets.' Jay said immediately.

'They look a bit like the animals Bertram and I saw in the woods after we left Salutem,' Chris said, 'only the ones we saw had stripes and bristles on them.'

'You saw wild pigs?' Jay's eyes were wide, 'they're supposed to be dangerous, aren't they?'

Chris shrugged, 'they ignored us, apart from this one little one who came over for a look at us. The mother didn't like the big feline grabbing one of her babies though, she ran at it and saw it off.' He could still see the jaguar in his mind, still feel the fear once they realised it had been stalking them.

'I should think she did!' Jay was shocked.

'Then, when we got to the river, Jax had to kill the jaguar cos it had followed us and was looking to kill one of us to eat!'

This had the desired effect on his friend. Horrified, Jay turned to him. 'I'd heard you belted Jax, everyone did, but I hadn't heard about the jaguar. Weren't you scared?'

'I was scared of everything at that point,' Chris admitted, 'I didn't know where I was or what we were doing, or where we were going. There were these strange people who wanted to take us on a floating thing and all I wanted was my mum.' His voice caught on the last word and he lowered his eyes, willing himself not to cry.

'I know mate,' Jay said quietly. 'Terrifying at first, isn't it? Seb and I were lucky in a way, we got out of Barlang and a hunting party found us almost immediately. They had food and water, which we hadn't even thought about of course, and they brought us back here with them. The boat ride was a bit interesting, made me feel ever so sick it did, wobbling about like they do. Seb was ok but he says I was green.'

Chris nodded, 'don't you miss your family though?' he asked.

'I do,' Jay admitted, 'but Seb and me had a chat and we decided that, as we were here and there was nothing we could do about getting them out, we have to make the best of our lives in Portum. In a way it's honouring our parents and our friends. I mean, being miserable all the time won't do anyone any good, will it?'

'No, I suppose not,' Chris said, 'but it would be great if we could find a way to go back and help others get out. I know there are quite a few folk in Salutem who would love to escape the caves.'

'Need a dragon for that mate,' Jay said, 'or a boat, and you're not getting me on one of those things again.'

Chris grinned, 'we'll have to get ourselves a couple of dragons then, won't we? Wonder how it feels to fly? I bet it's amazing!'

'Yeah, the rush of wind on your face, the sheer terror of being so high up, must be fantastic.' Jay said, his voice dripping with sarcasm.

Chris shook his head and decided to change the subject. 'What are those?' he asked, indicating lots of white shapes on the far side of the river.

'Those are sheep,' Jay said firmly, 'they have these fluffy coats which get cut off every year and that's where wool and yarn comes from to make cloth and jumpers and stuff.'

Chris gazed at the insignificant looking little white, fluffy blobs. 'Wow, all that from those little things? Amazing.'

They carried on walking until they were beyond the farms and trudging along the gravel banks of the now shallow river towards the towering cliffs and the cave Chris remembered Anilla taking him into.

They came round an outcrop of rocks and could see into the enormous bowl of the dragon's home. There were very few people around, but dragons could be seen, sunning themselves on the cliffs glittering in the sunlight.

'Wow,' breathed Jay, 'look at them, they're beautiful.'

Chris could only nod. Would he ever be considered for training as a rider he wondered? It seemed Jay was thinking the same thing.

'Wouldn't it be great, if they let us try standing at a hatching,' he said quietly, 'I mean, to get to ride one of those...' his voice trailed away as one of the beasts stretched its wings and dropped from the top of the cliff, beating its wings gently, lazily, it landed on the edge of the large lake in the centre of the bowl and, waddling comically, waded into the water until all they could see of it was its nose and the tip of its tail. Beneath the surface, they could see the scales glittering blue and green. 'Terrifying, obviously, but wouldn't it be great?'

'They take your breath away, don't they?' Chris said softly.

'Come on,' Jay said, dragging his eyes away from the bathing dragon, 'let's go see these eggs, shall we? Might be the only chance we have.'

'Jay,' Chris sighed, 'you know we'll get into trouble if we go in there. Even Anilla caught it from Fallaren when she took me in. We can't!'

'Oh come on.' Jay wheedled, 'we could be in and out before anyone sees us. Nobody knows where we are, no one's looking for us.'

'But still,' Chris countered, 'Taivas could tell her rider, and she's Anilla's sister, and then we'd cop for it.'

'Which one's Taivas?' Jay asked.

'She's huge and silver and seems to spend most of her time wrapped around her eggs.' Chris said testily.

'Huge and silver? You mean like that one over there?' Jay indicated a dragon heading for the lake, her rider astride her neck.

'Yeah, exactly like that one.'

'So she won't even know we've sneaked a peek at her eggs, will she?' Jay said eagerly. 'Oh, come on Chris, we'll be quick as quick can be, quicker even. Come on!'

Chris sighed heavily, 'Oh alright then, quick as we can. I hope Taivas doesn't mind, but she seemed to like me when I came with Anilla.'

Treading as quietly as they could, they crossed the river, gravel shifting under their feet and making what seemed like an unreasonably loud noise. They were almost at the cave now; they could feel the cool air drifting round their ankles as they walked towards the opening of the tunnel which would lead them to the clutch.

'Hope that was her we saw going for a bath,' Chris said nervously.

They crept forward as silently as their booted feet on the gravel would allow as images of what an upset dragon could do to them flitted across their minds.

'I'm not so sure this was a good idea,' Jay said, a gulp in his voice.

'Neither am I, but we're here now,' Chris replied

quietly.

'It feels like we shouldn't be here,' Jay said.

'We shouldn't,' Chris said, 'you know we shouldn't.'

'Oh, what are we doing?' Jay groaned, 'come on, let's go.'

'It was your idea! Anyway, we're almost there,' Chris said, 'just around that corner. Let's just have a quick look at them, then we'll leave. Alright?'

Curiosity got the better of Jay. 'Alright.'

They reached the corner and peeped around it. There before them lay the eggs.

'Wow!' Jay's soft exclamation whispered in echoes around the huge cave.

'They look different to when I was here with Anilla,' Chris said thoughtfully, 'look, they're glittering, like the cliffs outside in the sunshine.'

'Maybe it's because you saw them when they'd just been laid,' Jay suggested.

'Maybe.' Chris edged forward a little, tiptoeing towards the clutch.

'What are you doing?' hissed Jay, 'come back you idiot, you'll get us into trouble!'

Chris ignored him and edged closer to the nearest egg. It was a mottled bluey green and brown, and it looked so smooth. Without his realising what he was doing, he reached out a hand and gently stroked the egg. It was cool beneath his fingers, and smooth.

'Chris!' Jay hissed louder this time, 'come away

from there, we have to leave.'

Giving the egg one last gentle pat, Chris turned and scurried back to his friend.

'What were you thinking?' Jay looked horrified, 'what if you've hurt the baby dragon?'

'How could I have hurt it?' Chris asked, 'I barely touched the shell, I just stroked it. That can't harm it, can it?' He was leaning back against the smooth stone wall of the tunnel now, unthinkingly caressing the stone. 'This reminds me of Salutem,' he said suddenly, 'the clear, smooth stone walls, the way they make whispers carry.'

Jay looked at him quizzically.

'They had spies set on us,' Chris said, 'they used the walls to listen in on our conversations.'

'Why?' Jay demanded, 'what had you done?'

'Oh, not much, just planned revolution and mass escapes.' Chris grinned. 'Anyway they set this woman onto Bertram and me, and I found out because I leaned against the wall and hear her talking about us to some-one.'

Jay's eyes were goggling now. 'That's terrible.'

Chris was about to speak, then he froze as a voice was carried to him. 'Someone's coming!'

'Quick, let's get out of here.' Jay turned and was hurrying as quietly and quickly as his boots on the gravel would allow.

'Now, why didn't I think of that!' Chris said as he caught up with his friend.

They left the cave as quickly as they dared, checking constantly for sounds of returning dragons or riders. At the mouth of the tunnel they paused as a shadow passed and they saw the tip of a blue tail skim across the entrance. Keeping close to the wall, they waited. Then Chris peered out and around into the bowl.

'Come on, it's safe,' he whispered, gesturing for Jay to follow him.

They crossed the river, almost running back towards the nearest animal fields. Panting slightly, they leaned on the fence of the first pen they came to and found themselves face to face with the biggest pig they'd ever seen. It looked up at them, grunted enquiringly and, when they appeared to have no food for it, wandered away, its curly tail wiggling as it walked.

'I'm never doing that again,' Chris said, 'the next time I see a clutch of dragon eggs will be when everyone goes for the hatching. And next time there's a clutch in the cave, I'm staying well away!'

'Me too!' Jay said, 'I'd love to be a rider, but I don't think either of us is ready yet, we've not been here long enough. Give it a year or so.'

Chris nodded, 'I can't see them wanting us anywhere near a dragon yet,' he agreed, 'I'm still getting used to fresh air and no roof,' he joked.

Laughing, they wandered back towards the village.

***

Portum was busier than ever. More flags flew, from the traders' tents, from the council hall roof, from the boats on the river. Chris had to push through the crowds to get to the riverside. A long, flat-bottomed boat, similar to the one which Anilla had been in when he and Bert were rescued, was pulled up on the gravel and a crowd had gathered around the crew. Peering over shoulders, Chris could see a couple of bewildered, scared looking boys and a girl. They were pale and very thin.

'Looks like more newcomers,' he said over his shoulder to Jay, 'they look like me and Bert did when we got here.'

Jay struggled to see and pushed himself forward a little further. He caught a glimpse of the youngsters before they were hurried away by an older woman Chris didn't recognise.

'Where will they take them?' he asked.

'Probably to that place we were in at first,' Jay said, 'give them some time to rest and get used to the noise here.'

'Wonder where Bert is,' Chris said.

'He's here.' A hand landed on Chris' shoulder and he turned to see Bert grinning at him. 'What's going on?'

'Some new kids,' Chris said, 'Look just like we did when we got here.'

'Oh.' Bert looked around, 'busy isn't it. What a time to arrive!'

'I know, must be even scarier for them than it was for us.' Chris said. 'Where are you heading?'

'I need food,' Bert announced, 'coming?'

Chris and Jay nodded. 'I'm always up for food,' Jay said. 'Chris, you go find a table, I'll fetch you batu.'

Chris nodded and turned to survey the dining area. There were no free tables anywhere. He turned to find his friends, joining them in the queue to retrieve his own drink.

'There's nowhere to sit,' he told them.

'Have to be the beach then,' Jay said cheerily.

Bert raised an eyebrow at this, turning to glare at the crowded tables.

They moved away from the serving table, their hands full, and gave the dining area one last look before heading to the gravel beach a short distance away. They sat in a row, each shuffling in an attempt to get comfortable.

'Well, isn't this nice,' Jay said with forced cheerfulness.

'Not really,' Bert replied, 'but I'm so hungry I really don't care.' He was shovelling food into his mouth, taking gulps of his drink between mouthfuls.

Chris sat quietly, cradling his mug of batu, hands resting on his bent knees, gazing at the water. The sounds of Portum behind them rose and fell as he watched ducks bobbing about and, at the other side of the river, a boat pulled up, its passengers disembarking in cheerful chaos.

Bert and Jay finished their meals and picked up their own mugs, and the three of them sat in companionable silence, watching the action across the water.

As they sat there, they could hear snippets of the conversations going on around them. Two women discussing a man one of them liked, a couple of fishermen talking about pots versus nets, a third joined them and championed line fishing. Then a group of smith crafters sat at the nearest table, recently vacated by the two women. They began complaining about work and Bert's ears pricked up. He sat still and listened carefully.

'But he never listens,' one of them said, 'I went to him to ask about working for journeyman status and he just sent me packing.'

'Well, you never liked him much, did you?' his friend said, 'and you know how picky they are about who they choose to train up.'

'What about that new lad?' the first voice continued.

'Him that just got here from wherever it was?'

'Yeah, they're already talking like he's some great whizz. I bet he'll get picked before I do.'

Jay and Chris exchanged glances and looked over at Bert, who had gone pink.

'Doubt it, I heard his attitude puts them off. He's a bit full of himself.'

'He's good though.'

'Got to be able to get along with folks, it's not all about talent, not anymore. Time was when you were guaranteed a fantastic work life if you got into the smiths, now we've got so many we're full, if you ask me, but they keep bringing us more apprentices.'

As the voices carried on complaining, Chris and Jay looked across at Bert, whose face had gone dark red. He was staring determinedly at the river, obviously not seeing anything. Chris and Jay exchanged glances and Jay drew breath to speak but Chris silenced him with a slight shake of his head.

After a few more minutes the men who had been doing the complaining left.

'Quick, let's get that table,' Chris said, standing up. Jay beat him to the table, quickly clearing away the mess left by the previous occupants.

'You coming bro?' Chris asked, his head cocked on one side as he looked at his friend.

Bert shook himself back to the present and looked up. 'Yeah,' he said, standing reluctantly and walking with Chris to the more comfortable seats at the table. He sat down gingerly, then leant his elbows on the table and sagged.

'I'll go get some drinks.' Jay tactfully withdrew, leaving Chris to cope with the despondent Bert.

'Are you ok?' Chris asked quietly.

Bert just shrugged.

'I bet they're the sort who aren't happy unless they're moaning about something.' Chris said, trying to bolster Bert's confidence.

'I guess,' Bert said, his voice muffled by his arms.

'They did say you're talented,' Chris pointed out, 'a whizz I think they said, and they think, for all their complaining, that you're in line for promotion soon.'

Bert lifted his head and looked at Chris. 'You're right.' He said, although his voice wobbled and sounded most un-Bert-like. 'I have talent, I know that. I suppose it just never crossed my mind that I needed to get along with more people. It's not been a problem before, I got along with everyone in Salutem.'

'I know you did bro,' Chris said, 'but we all knew each other our whole lives, and that makes a difference. Here,' he waved his hand to indicate their current surroundings, 'we're strangers to them and we need to let them see who we are, we can't just assume they'll understand us, just like we don't always understand them.'

Bert nodded, surreptitiously wiping his eyes with the back of his hand. 'You're right,' he said, 'I know you're right. When did you get so wise?' He elbowed Chris in the ribs as he attempted to regain his composure. 'Looks like I need to work a bit harder on being sociable and make some friends cos I sure don't want anything to hold me back.'

Chris grinned, 'Of course you don't. You'll do great as a journeyman smith crafter.'

'Of course, my goal is to be a rider,' Bert's voice dropped to a whisper, 'then they'll lose me. But until then I'll work hard so they miss me when I'm gone!'

'Lose you?' Chris queried.

'Yeah, when I get a dragon.' Bert spoke as if explaining the obvious to a simpleton.

'But you don't...I mean, they won't lose you. You keep your craft.' Chris stammered, 'you get six months to do basic training, according to Anilla, then you go back to working part time.'

'Oh!' Bert deflated momentarily.

Jay returned bearing a tray with a jug of batu, mugs and a plate of snacks. 'I thought we might need some sustenance,' he said.

'We just ate!' Bert said.

'Jay is always hungry,' Chris chimed in. 'Always.'

Jay grinned good naturedly and helped himself to a handful of the crispy bites he'd brought.

'I really think I should be going,' Bert said, pushing himself to his feet. 'I think I'll look in on the stall the smiths are running, see if there's anything I can do to help out. Then there are a couple of things I need. I'll catch you later bro.' With that, he left.

Chris watched as Bert strode through the streets as if he owned them, head high, chest thrown out. He was walking against the general flow of people, but he didn't slow down at all, people moved aside to let him pass. He looked, Chris thought, every inch the leader. Time would tell.

'Well.' Jay was watching Bert's progress too, 'wonder if that little spot of eavesdropping might be the making of our Bertie.'

'Could well be,' Chris said thoughtfully, turning his attention to the batu and snacks in front of him. 'What are these?' He picked up one of the crispy items Jay had been munching on and tried it. It tasted salty and crunched pleasantly in his mouth. 'Hey, these aren't bad!' He picked up a handful and began eating them, one after another.

Jay quickly grabbed some for himself and sat quietly eating, looking around at the crowds with little interest.

'What's up with you?' Chris asked, 'you're not normally this quiet.'

'Oh, nothing really. Just... I think it was seeing those eggs, makes me realise what we missed by being stuck in the caves for so long, and what our futures might hold. I mean, being a rider would be great, but imagine the work!'

'I know,' Chris said, 'but it would be so exciting! Being able to fly wherever we wanted,' he sighed. 'The freedom Jay, imagine the freedom.'

They sat for a while, enjoying their snacks and batu, until a familiar voice called them. They both turned to see Anilla waving at them.

'Hi,' Chris shouted, waving back.

'Don't think that's what she wants mate,' Jay said, jumping up, 'come on, I think our presence is required by the lady.'

Chris joined him and they made their way over to Anilla, who was obviously excited about something.

'What's up?' Jay asked.

'You look happy,' Chris observed.

'They want me to stand,' Anilla squealed.

'For a dragon?' Chris looked delighted. 'That's amazing news Anilla.' He gave her a hug, which she returned enthusiastically.

'It is!' she said, 'I'm so excited. They want me to be a rider!'

'Can't say I'm surprised, really,' Jay put in, 'you're such a hard worker, and you're so helpful and lovely. Can't think of anyone better to have a dragon.'

Anilla blushed pink. 'Thank you Jay,' she said, giving his arm a squeeze.

'What happens now?' Chris wanted to know, 'do you have to get special training or something?'

Anilla nodded, 'yes, there's classes,' she explained, 'Fallaren likes everyone to be aware of what's involved before they get paired with a dragon, it's a lot of work.'

'So it won't be for this hatching then,' Jay said.

'Oh no, possibly the next one,' Anilla said, 'but that won't be too long, one of the Queens flew just before you got here, so she should be laying very soon.'

Chris and Jay exchanged looks. This was obviously another language. Anilla noticed their expressions and laughed.

'That means a Queen mated just before you got here, so her eggs will be ready to be laid in the cave soon. Then, a few weeks after that, baby dragons!' She giggled again. They had never seen her so happy.

'Best hope the current clutch have hatched before the next lot are ready to be laid,' Chris joked, 'or Taivas won't be too happy.'

'They're expecting the current clutch will hatch in the next week or so,' Anilla told them. 'We've never had an overlap before.'

'I wonder if we'll ever be chosen for dragon looking after classes,' Jay said thoughtfully.

'I would imagine you both will be,' Anilla said, 'I know Fallaren and Narilka are looking for people around your age who would be willing to pair with a dragon. They'll just want you to be properly settled here first, you're both still new and we know from experience that it takes a while to get used to the outside world. No point rushing things.'

They nodded, 'Makes sense,' Chris said, 'good to know we'll be considered though.'

'Of course you will!' Anilla looked shocked, 'they need people to be riders.' She glanced around before drawing them closer to her. 'I overheard the council elders, you know, the ones we saw last night, the ones with the cloaks?' The boys nodded. 'Well, I overheard them talking to Fallaren and Narilka about concerns over numbers of clutches and numbers of suitable folk to be riders. They think we're going to run out of people soon, then what will happen?'

'You mean that makes them more willing to scrape the bottom of the barrel and have us be riders?' Jay asked jokily.

'Is this going to be a big problem then?' Chris asked, his mind whirling.

'Yes,' Anilla said.

'Oh, cheers for that,' Jay responded but Anilla shook her head at him.

'I think there are real concerns about numbers,' she said, 'but what can we do? We can only have so many babies, and they only grow up so fast.'

'We'll have to find folk from elsewhere then.' Chris said.

'Like where?' Anilla asked, but she already knew the answer, it was written plainly in Chris' face. 'We can't Chris,' she said firmly, 'we can't.'

'Can't what?' Jay asked.

'He wants to send riders to Salutem and the other cave systems and force their leaders to let people out.' Anilla said.

'It would be perfect,' Chris argued.

'It's not possible,' Anilla insisted, 'don't you think Fallaren would have suggested it if it were?'

Chris sagged, 'I suppose so.'

The three of them spent the rest of the day together, wandering around the trader's stalls, haggling with them for the best prices. Chris and Jay found the finger protectors they needed, and Anilla bought some herbs. 'We can't get these round here,' she explained, stashing the bundle of herbs safely in the large bag which hung from her shoulder.

Jay managed to eat more sausages in bread buns. The trader he got them from told him they were named Hot Dogs, which confused the boys as they were assured there was no dog in the sausages. Chris discovered a sweet treat, cakes with holes in the middle. He watched the tradesman cooking them in a deep pan full of oil, then rolling each one in fine powdered sugar. He bought six to share with his friends, but once he'd eaten one, he went back for more.

A group of people were walking around the stalls and they caught Chris' attention. They were all tanned and well-muscled, well dressed too he thought. 'Who're they?' He asked Anilla through a mouthful of cake.

'They're riders,' Anilla told him, 'Mostly from Portum I think. I don't know all our riders personally, but they look familiar.'

Chris watched the group whilst he absently ate the rest of his treat and, equally absently, wiped his fingers on his trousers where they left sticky white marks.

'Look at him, he's miles away,' Jay said, nudging Anilla. 'Should we wander off and see how long it takes him to catch us up?'

Anilla was about to reply, but a new voice spoke, very close to them.

'What's your new boyfriend doing? He's wiped sugar all down his trousers. Oh, he must be a real catch.' Jorash was sneering as he looked at Chris.

'He's much better than you.' Jay said hotly, immediately sticking up for his friend.

'I doubt it.' Jorash said, looking Jay up and down. 'I have just been promoted. I am on my way to being a master in my craft and, if you listen to rumours, to being leader one day.'

'Good for you.' Anilla, her face bright red, turned on him. 'I hope that makes you happy Jorash, I really do. But as far as you making me happy, it's a non-starter. Chris is kind and funny and generous, all the things you're not. Now go away and leave me and my friends alone!'

Her strident voice made Chris spin round and also caught the attention of the group of riders, who strode towards the trio.

'Is everything alright here Anilla?' The tallest man asked, he had a deep voice and he sounded very much in charge.

'Everything's fine rider.' Jorash sounded more

nasal than usual and Chris noticed his face starting to colour.

'I was asking the lady,' the rider said, emphasising the last word and looking directly at Anilla.

'Jorash was being…his usual self.' Anilla said, with a small smile to the tall man. 'Thank you Dar.'

One of his fellow riders was now standing beside Chris. Glancing down at him she whispered, 'you've got something on your trousers my friend.'

Chris glanced up at her twinkling eyes then down at his trousers. 'Oh, thank you.' He said, dismayed to have been found fault with. He began rubbing at the marks but his hands were sticky and he was only making matters worse.

'Come over here a minute,' the rider said and led him away from the others and behind one of the stalls. 'Do you have a drop of water and a cloth I could borrow?' she asked the trader, who willingly supplied both. Chris found himself holding a damp cloth and being supervised by both the rider and trader as he cleaned himself up.

'Thank you,' he said in a small voice as he handed back the cloth once he'd finished.

'Come on, let's get back to the party,' the rider smiled, 'I'm Natalia, but folk call me Nat.'

'Pleased to meet you Nat,' Chris said, 'I'm Chris.'

'Not been here long?'

Chris shook his head, 'only a few weeks,' he told her.

'Thought so, you're still thin and weedy. At least

you're getting some colour now, can always tell the newbs by their skin.' She grinned at him, flashing white teeth.

They made their way back to Anilla and the others, where a first-class argument was in full swing.

Jorash, it seemed, had managed to insult everyone and was being shouted down by several riders, Jay and Anilla. Everyone was talking at once so Chris had a hard time following what was going on.

Nat asked one of her fellow riders who filled her in, then she turned to Chris. 'The tall, thin lad with the awful voice has said riders are a waste of time and resources and we don't need dragons,' she told him.

Chris gaped. 'He said that? To a group of riders? He's even more stupid than he looks!'

'He is,' Nat agreed, 'and Dar, Jake and the rest are making their own opinions heard, as you can see.' She grinned, 'I love a good fight, always makes a Gather interesting.'

'Does this kind of thing happen often?' Chris asked, watching in fascinated horror as Dar took a swing at Jorash.

'Oh yes,' Nat said happily.

Fallaren arrived, with Jax at his side, to see what the commotion was about, and began hauling riders away from the scrum that had formed around Jorash. Anilla and Jay were caught up in the middle of it and Chris saw Jay standing protectively in front of Anilla, trying to edge her out of the way.

'You should know better Dar,' Fallaren was saying, 'you keep out of trouble. You're a rider, you all are.'

'But he said riders are useless, a waste of time and resources,' Dar told Fallaren. 'We had to protect the honour of our kind.'

'Not like this.' Fallaren said shortly. 'Jax, take Jorash to the council hall please. Anilla, are you all right my dear? You look shaken.'

'I'm ok,' Anilla said, 'Jay looked after me.'

'Where's Chris?' Fallaren demanded.

'Behind you,' Anilla replied, 'with Nat.'

Fallaren spun around to see Chris, eyes wide, watching him. Nat by his side trying to look concerned about him. 'Chris!' The relief in his voice was obvious. 'Nat, thank you for looking after him.'

'My pleasure,' Nat said, giving Fallaren a casual salute, 'he's the one you've been talking about, is he?'

Fallaren nodded and Chris found himself the centre of the rider's attention.

'Bit weedy, but I'm sure he'll improve,' was Nat's judgement.

'Never underestimate a guy based on his build,' Dar warned her, 'look at Eva, she's strong, fierce and fearless and she's only about his size.'

'Good point,' Nat conceded, 'and he says he's not been here long.' She looked at Chris, nodding her approval. 'Yeah, Fallaren, if he comes over our way, we'll take care of him.'

Chris stared at her, then at Fallaren and Dar.

'Excellent! I thought that would be the case.' Fallaren sounded pleased. 'Now, enjoy the rest of the Gather, and no more fights please.' He looked directly at Dar, then walked off in the direction of the council hall.

'No doubt we'll be seeing you soon, Chris,' Dar said, patting him on the shoulder.

'Yeah, take care midget,' Nat said, grinning at him, 'see you around.'

The group wandered away, laughing amongst themselves. Dar looked over his shoulder at Chris and gave him a smile.

Chris turned his attention to Anilla and Jay, who looked as stunned as he was feeling.

'What just happened?' he asked.

'Well, I'd say Fallaren just let slip he's going to be putting you up for a dragon soon,' Jay said, glancing at Anilla for confirmation.

'I've only been here a couple of months, not even that really,' Chris knew he was babbling but as his nerves released he couldn't stop himself. 'Oh my, Anilla, if you go up for the next clutch, I might not be far behind you.' His face split in a huge grin at the thought.

'Yeah, I guess I'll be left behind.' Jay said in a small voice.

'I doubt it.' Anilla said briskly.

'Yeah, didn't you say they were getting desperate?' Chris grinned at his friend.

'Hey!' Jay tried to look offended and failed.

'I've had enough of this,' Chris indicated the stalls and crowds, 'shall we have a walk somewhere less crowded?'

'If that's possible,' Jay said.

'Yes, come on, this way,' Anilla turned and led them away from the stalls and the noise towards the main square.

It was quieter here; the tables were still full but the noise more subdued. Anilla led them past the dance square towards the council building and the bathing house. As they walked past the council hall they heard raised voices.

'Oh dear!' Anilla stopped dead in her tracks. Jay and Chris almost walked straight into her. 'Listen,' she whispered. From the hall came Fallaren's voice, he was yelling at someone.

'Someone's catching it,' Jay said.

'Presumably Jorash,' Chris said.

Anilla sighed and nodded. 'I had a lucky escape there,' she said.

Narilka's voice joined Fallaren's now, and Jorash could be heard whining plaintively. Loud footsteps approached the door and the three friends scuttled round the corner just as the main door was thrown open and Fallaren stormed out. Peeking around the corner of the building, Chris watched him striding towards the dining area.

'Shall we pop back to ours?' Jay suggested, 'you know, keep out of the way for a bit. You could try showing us how to make batu Anilla.'

Chris grinned and Anilla rose to the challenge.

'You're on!' she said, 'lead the way.'

***

As the sun began setting, they made their way back to the centre of Portum, ready for the feast to begin. They could already smell the roasting hog over the huge fire pit, and as they drew nearer, they could hear the sizzling of the meat as it dripped fat onto the fire.

Extra tables had been set out and Anilla quickly chose one, taking her seat and beckoning the boys to do the same. Once they were settled Chris asked, 'how does this work? I saw people paying for drinks last night, do we have to pay for our dinner tonight?'

'No silly,' Anilla laughed, 'this is being provided by us here at Portum. Our guests and all the folk who live here are welcome and we can all eat as much as we like.' She winked at Jay who had licked his lips. 'Just make sure you leave some for us please.'

They had got there just in time, the tables rapidly filled and, before long, the bell rang to signal the start of the feasting. Chris was about to stand up but Anilla put a hand on his arm.

'Tonight, we sit still,' she said, 'and the meal is brought to us. We did try letting everyone help themselves, but it was chaos. This way, everyone gets a share, and if there's any left, we can go help ourselves to it later.'

'Good.' Jay said, looking around. 'They can bring me as much as they like, I'm starving.'

'You've done nothing but eat all day!' Chris protested.

'I can't help it,' Jay laughed, 'hey, there's Seb!' He stood and waved at his brother, 'Seb, over here!'

Seb and the healer he was with both walked towards their table and Chris shuffled closer to Anilla to make room for them both. He noticed the bright pin Seb was wearing on his shoulder.

'Hey, congratulations,' he said, pointing out the pin to Jay, who immediately gripped his brother's arm firmly.

'Well done brother,' he said, 'you deserve it.'

'He does indeed,' said the other healer, 'he's worked so hard these last few weeks.'

'Thanks,' Seb looked embarrassed, 'this is Robin,' he introduced the older man, 'he's my supervisor at the infirmary.'

Robin smiled round at everyone. Chris was about to effect introductions when a pile of plates and cutlery was put on the table in front of him, followed immediately by the arrival of a long platter of meats and vegetables. He handed round the plates, saying everyone's name as he did so. Robin nodded at Jay and Anilla, then they all helped themselves to their meals and soon the silence around the table was broken only by the sound of cutlery being used.

'Oh my!' Jay said, giving his plate one final swipe with his last potato, 'that was delicious.'

'It is good, isn't it,' Anilla was still only halfway through her dinner.

Chris had almost finished his, he was already eyeing the food left on the platter, just as Jay reached over and began filling his plate again. 'Hey,' Chris said, 'remember there's other folk who want some more too!'

Jay guiltily dropped the potatoes he'd been about to put on his plate.

'It's alright. Jay, you can have mine,' Anilla said, 'I'm nearly full as it is.'

'Full?' Chris said, looking at her food, 'how can you be full? You've hardly eaten.'

'Ah, but I've been here for years,' she told him, 'I'm not fresh out of the caves. My body isn't recovering from insufficient food.'

'Fair, I suppose,' Chris said, 'but I'm getting there.'

'Indeed you are,' Anilla laughed, poking him in the ribs, 'now finish your dinner. Jay, don't worry, they'll come round and ask if anyone wants more if our platter is empty. You eat what you want.'

'He's a growing lad,' Seb put in, 'growing outwards that is!' He laughed as Jay glared at him. Both brothers ate heartily.

As the evening wore on the tables were cleared and the beer and wine began to flow. Several brewers and vintners had arrived in Portum and they were competing with Portum's own brewers for customers.

Musicians filed onto the stage and very soon the makeshift floor was full of couples. After a while, the formal music and dancing gave way to livelier stuff and Chris and Jay pulled a giggling Anilla onto the floor with them.

The sky darkened and the flares were lit. No one noticed the full moon hanging in the sky directly above them. Portum was full of laughter and dancing. Just for the moment, no one had any cares.

Chris wasn't sure when he first became aware of the noise. It vibrated his ears unpleasantly. He rubbed at them, shaking his head in irritation.

Anilla was rubbing her ears too, then she froze and looked around. Spotting Narilka, she shot away from Chris and Jay and they could see her speaking urgently to the leaders.

'What's got into her?' Jay asked.

'Not a clue,' Chris said, 'fancy a drink?'

Jay nodded and the pair were making their way to the Portum brewery table when Anilla caught up with them.

'There's no time for that now,' she told them breathlessly, 'come on, come with me.'

'Anilla! What's going on?' Chris demanded, irritated that he was being denied his drink.

'The hatching,' Anilla told him. 'The hatching's about to start. Come on, the dragons will start calling soon. Come on!' She ran and, after a moment's hesitation, Jay and Chris followed her. As they left the square a loud bellowing began and someone was ringing a bell. Immediately everyone stopped what they were doing and began hurrying in the direction of the dragon caves.

A flood of people moved towards the caves, Jay and Chris trotted along, following Anilla. They heard her being greeted by another young woman, a taller version of herself.

'That must be her sister,' Chris panted, 'she's the rider of the mother dragon.'

Jay nodded. 'Yeah, she must be excited, her first

babies.'

'Hadn't thought of it like that.'

Everyone flowed into the cave and immediately all chatter stopped. Soon the tiered seating was filling up. Anilla took a seat with Fallaren and Narilka on the second tier and she waved Jay and Chris to seats immediately in front of her. Further along to his right, Chris could see Bert, sitting with the other smiths. He was leaning forward eagerly, not taking his eyes off the eggs. As the last people straggled in and found seats the bellowing from the male dragons stopped.

All attention was focussed now on the clutch. The mottled eggs with their strangely glittering shells were still protected by the curl of their mother's tail. Anilla's sister was standing next to Taivas, stroking her neck and head, talking to her.

The first egg moved jerkily and there was an indrawn breath from the watching crowd.

'How long does this take?' Chris whispered to Jay, who shrugged, not taking his eyes off the eggs.

A group of young people was led in by one of the riders. They formed a loose semi-circle around the eggs and watched nervously as the rocking movements increased. Cries could now be heard from the baby dragons still trapped in their shells.

After what felt like an age, the first egg cracked and the baby dragon struggled out. It flopped wetly onto the sandy floor and lay there, crying for a moment before righting itself to stand on wobbly legs. Its damp skin was translucent. Chris stared in wonder as it made unsteady progress towards the waiting youngsters. It stopped in front of one boy, looked at him closely, then moved on to the next. Here it stopped, looked directly at the lad's face and flapped its wings weakly. Chris was reminded of the young chickens he'd helped with back in Salutem. The chosen boy however looked very happy, he raised a hand to the weedy looking neck and stroked it, the baby crooned.

Chris turned in his seat and grinned at Anilla. 'This is great,' he whispered before turning back in time to see the second dragon hatch.

This one sprang from the shell energetically and almost ran to the line of waiting hopefuls. It looked around for a moment before poking its nose gently at a young girl. She gazed up in wonder before reaching tentatively to stroke the soft, damp nose. The dragon was making happy noises at her, and the girls face broke into a delighted grin.

As Chris watched, one by one the eggs hatched and the dragons chose their human partners. One of the larger eggs was rocking now and a crack appeared along the side of the shell. Slowly, the crack widened and a snout appeared, followed quickly by the head and neck. This dragon looked bigger than the others. It took its time leaving the egg, by the time it was standing on the sand its scales were drying and their colour was showing, this was a silver dragon. She shook her wings and folded them against her back before strutting forward, straight to a dark-haired girl. The dragon squawked impatiently at her and the girl laughed, Chris heard her talking to the dragon, telling her to have a little patience and she would be fed soon.

Anilla tapped him on the shoulder and whispered,

'that's my cousin! We have two riders in my family now!' When Chris looked at her, she was glowing with pride.

There was just one egg left now, the egg Chris had patted earlier in the day, it was rocking but no cracks had appeared yet. He felt a surge of guilt, was he wrong to touch the shell? Had he, as Jay had suggested, harmed the little dragon inside?

Then, as he watched, the shell split in two and the dragon fell out. It sprawled onto the sand and lay for a moment, blinking, then it was on its feet and looking around. It stumbled straight past the line of potential partners and began looking up into the seating, crying. Chris looked guiltily at Jay, who shrugged. He glanced around, there were concerned faces everywhere.

'What happens if it doesn't find a partner?' he asked.

'Goes wild I think,' Jay said, not taking his eyes off the dragon.

'That's bad.' Chris said, watching the baby dragon carefully. Surely, he hadn't done any harm to the baby, he'd only stroked the shell.

The young dragon seemed to be looking for someone. Then it turned its head towards Chris and he found himself staring into a rainbow. He felt joy like he'd never known and was aware, in some dim way, that his life would never be the same again. Standing, he stumbled down the stairs to the dragon. His dragon. He gently stroked the neck and patted the nose, reassuring the dragon that all was well.

Around him pandemonium broke out. Voices were calling for him to be removed, for the dragon to be forced to find a different partner, or worse. The noise and confusion in the cave roused Taivas. Not usually protective of the young once they were hatched, she hadn't been taking any notice of the humans, until they began threatening her offspring. She almost ran towards the seating and reared up, wings spread wide, as she bellowed her fury at the angry people.

Fallaren was calling to other riders to come forward. Nat and Dar came leaping down the steps, calling to their friends to join them.

Without his noticing, Chris was surrounded by a protective ring. The riders stood with their backs to Chris and the baby dragon, facing the crowds. Fallaren was speaking urgently to Narilka and casting worried looks at Chris, who was oblivious.

ABOUT THE AUTHOR

Kate Ridley

Kate Ridley is a coffee fuelled, animal loving fantasy fiction writer. Born in York, she lived in North Yorkshire for most of her adult life, with brief periods living in Madeira, before re-locating to Derbyshire where she now lives with her partner, their daughter and two mad rescue dogs.
When she's not writing or cooking up plots, Kate spends her time reading, listening to music, baking, gardening and walking.
Portum is her first book, the start of an adventure series for young adults.